DISTRACTION

Elyse Rundell

DISTRACTION

Elyse Rundell

Elyse Rundell

ISBN: 9798376852293

To my momma in heaven…

Thank you for leaving your "trashy" romance novels around the house for a teenage girl to steal and read. I'm sure your face would be as red as a beet while reading this book… but deep down you would love it! Oh, my lands!

Elyse Rundell

Chapter 1

"Where would you like my load?" The gorgeous stranger groaned as he wiped the sweat with a bandana from his tan, muscled neck.

"Anywhere you'd like…" I murmured, stepping closer, biting my lip in anticipation.

"Anywhere?" he asked, reaching over and dragging his finger along the collar of my V-neck shirt.

"Anywhere…" I purred as he dipped his finger into my cleavage, heaving with every ragged breath I took.

"Anywhere?" he asked again, dragging that same sinful finger down, dipping it into the waist of my jeans.

"Anywhere," I breathed…

"Kelly!? What do you mean anywhere? Where can I drop this load of mulch?" called the delivery driver from the window of his dump truck.

"Shit. Sorry, Hector!" I shook my head to clear my mind of the daydream and pulled my cap further down on my head. "On the tarp at the bottom of the hill," I shouted the instructions and walked back towards the barn. *I've got to get laid...* I thought to myself just as my phone rang. *Oh, for fuck's sake.*

"Hey, Nik" I answered, putting on a more cheerful persona.

"How are you?" she responded without even saying hello. Nikki was never one to beat around the bush.

I sighed... that question did not grate on my nerves before my husband died. *How are you?* Now, it was like nails on a fucking chalkboard... even when it came from my younger sister.

"I'm good! We're booked solid through fall and next summer is already starting to fill up. Plus, I've been able to hire a full-time housekeeper," I knew this would not fully answer Nikki's question, but I wasn't in the mood for a heavy, emotional conversation. I was more interested in getting back to my daydream from earlier. "My schedule should be clearing up soon if you and Bryan wanted to come up for a visit."

There was a pregnant pause while my sister collected her thoughts. See... it's been a little over a year since Jake, my husband of twenty-seven years, died from cancer, and my family and friends still had kid gloves on when it came to my well-being. "We'll come up soon," she finally answered. "Are *you* doing okay? I can't believe it's been a year already."

Ha! Already? Some days it felt like it had been a decade... but then some days it felt like it was yesterday. I gave myself another mental shake before continuing, "Like I said, I'm good! It *is* hard to believe that a year has passed, but I'm making it. Besides... Sam is on her way to spend some time, so she'll be a welcome distraction."

"Distraction... for sure," she laughed. "Y'all have fun and tell her hi for me. Love you, bye!"

"Love you too..." I chuckled as the phone disconnected.

Samantha "Sam", my very best friend since junior high school, would be here later today from Texas, and I could barely contain my excitement. Jake and I had moved to the Olympic Peninsula in Washington from Texas ten years ago to escape the sweltering heat and humidity, so it was always nice to have guests from home. Besides, a distraction was exactly what I was needing and 'my ride-or-die since junior high' was just what the doctor ordered.

I had a little time before I had to head to the ferry landing, so I figured a walk would help pass the time. Luckily, my favorite walk was just outside my door. KJ Farms (my take on a bed-and-breakfast) was spread out over my ten-acre piece of Pacific Northwest paradise. Private cabins were tucked away into secluded spots among the ferns and evergreen trees with walking trails for the guests that snaked around the property and through the gardens. It was close to everything the Peninsula had to offer... lavender farms, wineries and breweries, whale-watching tours, the Olympic National Trail for cycling, the mountains for hiking, the ocean and rivers for kayaking and fishing. Jake and I had worked so hard to get the farm to what it was. I'm not sure if it's the years of hard work, the great summer temperatures, or the breathtaking scenery, but I loved it and could not imagine living anywhere else. I waved to Larry, my property manager, and walked over to remind him of my day's schedule.

"Mornin', Larry!" I shouted through the fence, glad for the shade of my cap. People always assume that the Pacific Northwest is overcast and rainy, but we're in a rain shadow here on the northern tip of the Peninsula and get a ton of sunshine. "What kind of trouble are you drummin' up over here?"

"Morning, Kelly," he called as he returned my wave and walked over. "Just checking on the goats. I think we'll need to add another two or three pretty soon… at least." The goats were a favorite among our guests, but Larry had more of a love/hate relationship with them.

"Sounds good," I laughed, watching as the kids hopped around and head-butted one another then turned on Larry. "I'll make some calls later. I'm leaving for the ferry terminal to get Sam. You need anything while I'm out?"

"Dammit," he griped as he swatted at the more aggressive baby goat. "Just a foxy red-head and a big ass steak," he chuckled, making his belly jiggle as it poked through his suspenders. He always joked that he would play Santa if he could grow a better beard.

"Would you settle for a dark-haired lesbian and a greasy burger?" I teased with a wink.

Larry threw back his bald head, laughing so hard his cap fell off behind him. He reached down quickly and snatched it just before the goat made it a snack. I loved making that old man laugh. Larry was only in his late fifties, but he looked like he was pushing seventy due to his years of hard living. He was a workhorse though and could run circles around me, even though I was a few years younger. "Hell, I'll take what I can get," he crowed.

"You better not let Rosy hear that," I laughed. "I'll bring you back a burger," I threw him a kiss then turned to head to my jeep. "Bye, handsome! Be nice to the guests while I'm out."

"You wish!" he yelled.

I laughed and shook my head, then flipped him my middle finger as I climbed into the jeep. He was right. I *did* wish he was nicer to the guests but having a grumpy caretaker didn't seem to hurt business. Besides, Larry was my right-hand and had made this last year not quite as painful as it could have been. He lived in one of our cabins as part of his salary, so he was always there when I needed him... plus his on-again-off-again relationship with a local named Rosalie entertained me to no end.

Thirty minutes later I pulled into the parking lot for the Bainbridge Ferry just as it was pulling into the dock. Walk-ons are let off first, so I congratulated myself on my time management skills. In no time, I saw Sam walking with those disembarking, wheeling her suitcase waving like a lunatic. I nearly fell jumping out of the jeep. Tears started pouring down our faces when we hugged.

"Oh God! I can't believe I'm crying. It's just SO good to see you!" I sobbed, crushing Sam's bony shoulders as I squeezed her tight.

"It's been too long. I should have come sooner," she sobbed back squeezing me just as tight. We normally weren't this emotional, but these were not normal times.

I took a deep breath and shook my head. "Alright... let's get it together. I'm done with the tears," I fanned my face, thankful that I decided against mascara. "Whoo! Let the fun begin!" I cheered then gave her a look-over. "My friend... you are looking good!" I cooed, standing back to take her all in.

Sam did a twirl and patted the bottom of her short, dark bob. "Thanks! Looking good, feeling good, right? Now speaking of looking good! Holy cow, mama!" She snapped her fingers while I performed her same twirl adding some hand flourishes.

"Thank you! I've taken up yoga this last year and love it," I beamed. I was still a full-figured woman, but between losing weight these last couple of years (the only good side effect of my grief), farm work, and yoga... I was in the best shape of my life.

"Well, it loves you too. Now you just need to find someone who'll appreciate that smoking hot bod." Sam wiggled her eyebrows with her last statement.

"Ha! I don't know about how smoking hot it is, but I'm pretty proud of myself." I touched the corners of my eyes before adding, "Though, I keep some pudge as natural collagen. I don't need Botox that way." We laughed and loaded into my jeep as Sam described her latest debacles with Botox and microblading. *Growing older can be painful!*

The drive home, winding through the trees and around the different waterways, let Sam update me on her latest flings. She had been married to her college sweetheart for almost ten years, before they divorced, *both* deciding they preferred their same sex over each other. It was wild! She's been living her best, single, lesbian life ever since, being close with her ex-husband and his partner, having a great relationship with their kids and now even a couple of grandkids... one big, happy modern family.

"Have you lined up anyone for me while I'm here?" she asked with a wicked twinkle in her eye.

"Girl... my pimpin' skills are rusty," I chuckled. "*Though...*" I drug out the word, giving Sam my most mischievous grin, "I *may* have someone in mind, but you'll just have to wait and see. I don't want to jinx it!" A local brewery was providing beer for our crab boil that weekend, and I was betting their beer rep would be right up Sam's alley. "But on a similar topic... I have a job for *you* this weekend. Are you up for a challenge?" I gave her a half smile and wiggled my brow.

"I'm always up for a challenge... as long as it's about you and not me. Spill it," she demanded.

I took a deep breath. *Here goes nothing.* "I need you to use your keen powers of observation to see if I should fuck Erik."

Sam had chosen that moment to take a large gulp of her water, which ended up spraying across the console of my jeep. "Oh shit! Sorry!" she choked out amid a coughing attack. "You mean Erik, the guide guy, your best customer, Jake's *best* friend? *That* same Erik?"

"That's the one. He's up for it, and I think he could be just what I need. I sound crazy, right?" I would think I was crazy if I was her, which is why I needed an honest second opinion before I did something I would regret… and I don't like to have regrets.

"Alright, let's backup. Remind me again how he came into the picture."

Chapter 2

Five years ago...

Where the hell are they? I had driven by the drop pin for the trailhead that our newest guest had sent me three times, but no one was there. Parking was almost non-existent in the tiny parking lot that was right off the highway, so it was nearly impossible with my passenger van and trailer. The fourth time was a charm as I pulled up again and saw the group with their mountain bikes. My rig took up the entire parking lot, but at least I was off the road. Plus, I had a great view of the cyclists that had pulled in and were slowly dismounting. I was a married woman, but I wasn't blind. The tight biking shorts didn't leave much to the imagination. One in particular was just getting off his bike and had the best legs of the bunch. His bike shorts hugged every muscle of his thigh, and you could almost make out the line of his… I caught my breath and jerked my head up looking into the smirking eyes of the bicycling god. He sauntered over to the truck with that same panty-dropping smirk, his deep-set brown eyes crinkled with amusement.

"Hello, KJ Farms… are you enjoying the view?" he asked smoothly in the most delicious English accent, and I was a sucker for an accent.

"Jury is still out," I laughed, though on the inside I was dying of embarrassment. "Do y'all need any help loading up?" My husband usually made these transport runs for guests, but he hadn't been feeling well so I volunteered.

"We've got it… we'll just be a bit!" he called out as he walked back to the trailer with a chuckle.

"*We'll just be a bit,*" I said in my attempt at an English accent. "*We'll just be a bit,*" this time with a mixture of English and my Texas twang. "*We'll just be a bit,*" this time a little deeper trying to match his voice.

"Are you mocking me?" It was that same delicious accent. I had forgotten that the windows were rolled down. Was it too late to go running and screaming into the forest? I looked over as he was climbing into the passenger seat. He still had that sexy smirk on his face so at least I knew he wasn't offended… at least he didn't *look* like he was offended.

"N–no. I like your accent. I was just being silly." I was not a person that was easily embarrassed, and I had already embarrassed myself twice within five minutes of being around this man.

"Your accent is fun too... *We'll just be a bit, pilgrim,"* he said the last part in a John Wayne-ish voice making us both laugh. "I'm Erik. I guide this pack of arseholes." He gestured toward the back of the van as the other riders were loading up, their equipment securely fixed on the trailer. They all murmured greetings in varied levels of weariness. "Which daughter are you?"

"Daughter?" I asked, sounding as puzzled as I felt... then realization dawned. "Oh, holdup! Do you think Jake is my DAD?' I burst out laughing as soon as the last word crossed my lips. "Whoo! I might need you to repeat that so I can record it for proof." I glanced over and saw that Erik had no idea why I was reacting this way. "Sorry. Jake is my *husband.* I'm Kelly." I glanced in the rearview mirror and realized that my blonde pigtails, cap, t-shirt and jeans made me look younger than my husband who was completely gray and mature beyond his years.

"Fuck," he hissed. "I don't suppose you could keep this exchange between us?" he asked sincerely. "I really like Jake and don't know if he'd appreciate me flirting with his wife." I bet that damned smirk gets him out of all sorts of trouble. *Flirting?* It made me laugh. I had always been a flirt myself, but it was nice for my self-confidence to hear that he was flirting back. I pulled onto the highway and headed back towards the farm.

"My lips are sealed. I wouldn't want to hurt his feelin's anyway. I'll just bask inwardly in the glow of the compliment." I glanced over and met his smile with my own.

17

"Bask away, just don't hurt his *feelin's.*" I could tell that he was joking with my accent, but a current of truth lay underneath regarding Jake's emotions. I liked him immediately.

"Like I said, my lips are sealed," I smiled. "Thank you so much for the bookings! So how will it work? You'll bring different groups, the same group or what?" My curiosity was taking over and there was still an hour and a half of a drive ahead of us. Erik had booked cabins with us for every other weekend for the next three months, so I was intrigued.

"I offer my guide services to other cyclists, kayakers, or hikers for set weekends. It depends on the type of trip they want. We'll usually go for the day, then come back to stay at the cabins, and head to a different trailhead the next day. Other times we might take our tents for overnights. It really depends…" Erik continued on with the details for most of the trip back to the farm. He didn't strike me as someone who would be so chatty, so it was interesting to see that he could be so animated. One could easily see how much he enjoyed what he said was his side hustle, only briefly mentioning being a graphic designer during the work week.

Jake was waiting for us when we pulled up the long driveway back at the farm. I crossed my fingers hoping that meant he felt better. Our place ran so much smoother when he was at the helm.

"How'd it go?" he asked as everyone climbed out of the van. The group kept their bikes on the trailer, since they were scheduled to go back out in the morning. "Kelly didn't talk your ear off too much, did she?" This last question was aimed in Erik's direction. I rolled my eyes at Jake while others reacted.

"Ha! Erik didn't shut up the whole time!" one of the guys in the group yelled.

"Yeah, I didn't know he could talk that much," said another one of the... what did Erik call them? Assholes. Seemed fitting.

"I told you they were arseholes," Erik quietly said so only Jake and I could hear. I laughed at our similar thoughts. Louder he continued, "It was great, Jake. Hope you're feeling better."

"I am. Just needed some rest. Y'all are welcome to come have a drink with us later. We'll be back on the deck," Jake motioned toward our house. The guest cabins were on the other side of the farm. "Just come on back if you'd like, there's a gate on the side."

"I'll do that," Erik leaned in closer to us both, "but just me. I need a break from these wankers." We all laughed, and I left Erik and Jake to make plans for later.

I was lounging on our back deck having toked it up with Jake and now well into my second cocktail, when Erik walked through the side gate. Needless to say, we were feeling no pain.

"Jay–ake! Your new best friend is here!" I shouted in an animated voice to my husband who was in the kitchen playing bartender. He had been singing Erik's praises for the last hour, so I couldn't resist being snarky.

"Are you pissed already?" Erik asked, taking a seat in the chair opposite me with that same sexy smirk as before. *Does he have resting-sexy-face?* I laughed at my own joke then responded to Erik's question.

"Pissed? No way," *Why would he think I was pissed?* "I'm high… a little tipsy, but not pissed… Why would I be pissed?" I asked aloud that time.

"Sorry, I meant drunk. Thanks, mate," he said to Jake as he handed him his vodka cocktail laughing at my confusion.

"Oh, ha ha," I said sarcastically, "So tell us more about you, Er–ik. Married? Kids?" I eyed him suspiciously. "Ex-MI6 agent who is on the run from the law because you were framed for a murder and you're trying to clear your name?" I asked, crescendoing until the end for dramatic effect.

"Someone has an active imagination," he chuckled. "Married, no kids, and not running from anyone. Is she always this nosy?" He directed the last question to Jake as he sat down next to me on the couch. It was another beautiful summer night on the Olympic Peninsula and the sun was just beginning to set.

"Oh yeah. I should have warned you." Jake laughed.

Erik smiled and glanced around. "It is so peaceful here, so calming. If I lived here, I'd never leave."

"That's why owning a bed-and-breakfast is perfect for us… everyone comes to us, and we don't have to go anywhere," I laughed.

Eric's Assholes from the guide had made it sound like he was the quiet, brooding type from some of the comments I heard, but that didn't seem to be the case. Erik chatted amicably about his life in Seattle. His wife of two years was named Catherine, and she was not a fan of his guide job. No children with no plans for any. He was the youngest of five siblings who all still lived in England close to his mother, whom he talked to often. Graphic design paid his bills but doing anything outdoors was his passion.

We spent the evening talking, laughing, and drinking until I could barely keep my eyes open, so I left Jake and Erik to their male bonding while I went to bed. Our pattern was formed.

Elyse Rundell

Chapter 3

Present Day...

"And that's how it began," I smiled at Sam from across the jeep. "Erik still hangs out with us after his trips and his clients sometimes do too. The nightlife on the Peninsula ends around eight, so pickin's are slim when looking for an adult beverage and a good time."

"And Erik still comes out a lot?" Sam asked, eyeing me as I answered.

I was glad that she was taking me seriously and not just brushing my craziness under the rug. "Yep. He has a standing reservation for a couple of cabins every other weekend, but he usually stays in one of the guest rooms there, in the big house, with me, so he can use both cabins for clients. He's been doing that for years now even when it's the off-season," I rattled all in one breath.

Sam paused for a moment and stared at me as I focused on the road. "And he's open to fucking *you*?" she asked, looking at me skeptically. I laughed at the expression on her face.

"Shut up," I grinned, "Is that too much of a stretch? We've been flirty with each other since the day we met, but it was *always* harmless." I took a deep breath and shrugged. "I thought he was joking at first, but he sounds serious. I'm thinkin' I'll just go for it."

She looked at me for a moment before hollering, "You go, girl!" Sam snapped her fingers. "Isn't he like... twenty years younger than you? Dammmmnnnn!"

I rolled my eyes. At least this reaction was better than the spitake from before. "He's thirty-four so not quite, but we have a good time together, so age is just a number... in my opinion." I leveled Sam with a side-eyed glance and a mischievous grin.

"And you don't mind the age difference?" Sam asked, still sounding skeptical. I didn't blame her one bit for not believing me. I might not believe me if I were her, plus I've always been a bit over-confident for my own good. This was a good reason why the fewer people that knew the better. Everyone would think I had gone off the deep end, trying to bag such a younger man.

"I shouldn't have said anything and just waited to see what you thought at the end of your visit," I said, shaking my head. "Like I said, I'm *thinking* about it, but I don't want to make a fool out of myself... at least no more than I normally do." I snickered trying to lighten the mood.

"What's there to think about?" Sam asked in disbelief. "If you're sure he wants to then why not go for it?"

I sighed after a second, "I'm looking for a distraction right now... from my grief... from life." I glanced over and smiled at Sam before continuing. "I'm only afraid he might be too much of a good thing. I'm not ready to settle down just yet, and I don't want to get attached."

"What? Why *not* get attached?" Sam eyebrows were raised in question. I knew Sam would tell me to jump Erik's naked body the first chance I got and not look back, but this attachment stuff was not like her.

"Who are you and what have you done with my friend Sam?" I laughed. "Okay... no judgment... but I want to slut it up for a while. Variety is the spice of life, right? I want to take some test drives before I buy another car... Try some appetizers before I settle on the entree... Sample the goods before I–,"

"I get it! Enough analogies," Sam snorted. "You won't hear any slut-shaming from me. God only knows," she laughed. "So, Erik will be one of your test drives?"

"Hopefully a recurring one if our chemistry is any indication," I leered in Sam's direction. "I just need your honest opinion once you meet him. Should we just remain friends or should I fuck him and screw the consequences because I'm horny as hell?"

"I'm leaning toward the latter, but I'm open to changing my mind," Sam replied.

"Honesty is all I need," I promised, "and an orgasm from someone besides my vibrator."

We both laughed and spent the rest of the drive discussing our latest sex toy finds.

Hours later, Sam and I were each kicked back on lounge chairs on my back deck enjoying some sparkling wine. Jake built this massive, engineered-wood monster for me right after we bought the property, and it's my favorite place. The deck wrapped around the back of our house, overlooking the evergreen forest and babbling creek. A wooden pergola covered an outdoor living space on one side with a seating area, fireplace and hot tub. The dining table and lounge chairs were outside the sliding door with nothing above but the sky. If I'm at home, I'm either in the kitchen or out here.

Sam and I had already covered the basics: our kids, our family, her job, the farm. She kept nagging me for hints about who I had lined up for her. Knowing Sam, she would drive me bonkers unless I gave her some more information.

"Okay! I invited someone to the crab boil Saturday who I think you'll like. Can that be enough to get you off my back?" I pleaded.

"Is she cute?" she asked, her mood was noticeably more cheerful.

I rolled my eyes, "Of course she is."

"I won't say another word about it then," she promised. "What happened to Erik's wife? I'm assuming she's no longer in the picture."

"They divorced about a year after we met," I stopped for a moment thinking back. "I actually only met her the one time, but it happened to be the night when it all fell apart." I took another big slug of my wine and poured myself another, topping Sam's off as well.

Her eyes widened in surprise as she took a large drink of hers, "Go on…"

Elyse Rundell

Chapter 4

Four years ago...

"I don't know why I'm so nervous. It's not like I care if she likes us or not," I yelled to Jake from the bathroom. Erik was coming in for the weekend and bringing his wife, Catherine, instead of one of his normal groups of Assholes.

"You're probably just nervous for Erik. I think he's hoping that she'll like *you* so much that she'll want to start coming out with him," Jake sighed, leaning against the door frame. "I'm afraid their happiness rests in your hands."

"Ha ha ha," I said as Jake laughed and walked away. "You have jokes. No pressure, Kelly. You're just responsible for saving the marriage of your husband's BEST FRIEND!" I heard Jake's laughter continue as he left the house. "Bastard. We've never even met this woman, and I'm supposed to make her love me." It was strange that we'd grown so close to Erik over this last year, and I had yet to meet his wife. Jake had met her once in passing when he went to Seattle for a Mariners game. He was not able to form much of an opinion in the limited time they interacted, except to say that she was 'hot'. I had complimented him on his use of adjectives and was still clueless about Catherine (though 'hot' *did* perfectly describe her after my deep dive search on social media.)

I grabbed my favorite cap, so I wouldn't have to fix the mess of blonde hair on my head and gave myself a mental shake. *No need to be nervous.* I only wanted Erik to be happy, and I was determined to keep an open mind. Apparently, he and Catherine were having issues and Erik felt like they were at a fork in the road… stay together or end it. Erik confided all this in Jake a few weeks ago. This weekend was going to be the deciding factor. *Maybe that's why I was a bundle of nerves.*

I found Jake outside warming up the grill. We were not only making dinner for Erik and Catherine but Larry and Rosalie and June and Daryl, a neighbor couple to whom we were close. They were already milling around our stone patio we use when having bigger parties at the farm. "I've got the sides ready to go. When are the happy couple supposed to arrive?" I asked Jake while reaching over and giving his ass a squeeze.

Jake gave me a side-eye glance, "Watch it... they should be here any minute."

"I promise to be on my best behavior... as long as they get here soon. I'm starving!" I smiled and went over to mingle with our other guests.

"Let's go ahead and eat. I'm not waiting for them anymore," Jake said, once they were about an hour late. "The steaks are done. Erik had said they were running a little late, but he hasn't answered his phone since."

"Now I'm worried. They could be wrapped around a tree or some–," I stopped as headlights shone coming up the driveway. "Thank you, baby Jesus. Let's eat!" We all cheered in agreement and grabbed plates as Jake went to greet the late arrivals as they pulled up. Our table was quiet as we started eating, so the raised voices from the driveway were easy to overhear.

"I don't think it's asking too much to get settled before we eat. *You're* the one that drug me out here to the middle of nowhere!" snapped a female voice.

"We're already late. Let's eat and have a bit of a chat, then I'll take you and the bags down. Let's not make this an issue," Erik seethed. My first impression of Catherine was off to a rocky start. We continued eating quietly around the table making awkward eye contact as we listened.

"*You're* the one making it an issue! We can eat but I need to go to the cabin as soon as possible," she demanded. Erik must have agreed since they both walked around the corner and up to our table with Jake.

"Hey everyone," Erik smiled and waved to the table. "This is my wife, Catherine. Catherine, this is Kelly, Jake's wife, Larry and Rosalie, and Daryl and his wife June. Sorry we're so late." I watched Catherine's face as Erik introduced her to everyone, but she looked as if she'd rather be anywhere else. My impression of her fell another notch. She *was* gorgeous with long, auburn hair that hung halfway down her back. Her skin was flawless and beautiful. I would not have been surprised if she stepped right out of an REI catalog since her outerwear was pristine.

"Nice to meet everyone," she said quietly with a shy smile. She must not have known we could hear her from the driveway. It's not like I expected her to be my favorite person or anything, but her likability was plummeting minute by minute.

"Nice to meet you," I replied along with everyone else. "Plates are here, so help yourself," I smiled. The old adage 'fake it til you make it' flashed in my head as the silence stretched around the patio. She and Erik fixed their plates and joined us at the table. *I better get the ball rolling.* "So, Catherine, what do you do in Seattle?"

"I'm a nurse at the Children's Hospital," she replied.

"Oh wow. I bet that can be interesting. Do you enjoy it?" I asked with a smile.

"It can be tough, but it's fine," she said. We all waited a moment thinking that she would elaborate, but she took another bite of her pasta salad.

"Erik says you enjoy living in the city. What kinds of things do you like to do?" I gave her another smile.

"Lots of things," she shrugged, "I didn't realize I would be getting the third degree," she said before taking another rather large mouthful of pasta salad and never looked up from her plate. I couldn't tell if she was meaning to be rude or was just that bad at conversation. *Kill her with kindness.*

"Sorry. I *am* pretty nosy. You'll enjoy the Peninsula even more tomorrow when it's light and you can see the scenery, though the stars are fantastic," I commented, trying to keep the conversation flowing, but not asking her a question directly.

"I've been here before, just not… to *your* place," she looked around as she said the last few words, with a hint of unpleasantness in her upturned nose. "I'm sure it's better in the light."

My eyebrows shot up making my eyes huge. *What in the actual fuck? Did I need to slap a bitch?* Jake placed his hand on mine and gave a squeeze knowing I was hanging on to my composure by a thread.

Erik's voice cut through the silence before I had a chance to respond. "It's my favorite place on the whole damn Peninsula, Catherine. How about you show a little more respect to our hosts?" My eyes grew even bigger. Rekindling their romance was looking like an impossible feat.

"How about *you* show a little more respect to your *wife?"* she shot back. Catherine stood up abruptly, sending her chair flying back. "I'm walking to the cabin," she announced and stomped off back towards the driveway.

"Sorry, everyone. I didn't mean for us to ruin the night," Erik sighed. He got up and righted his wife's chair.

"She doesn't have a clue where she's going. I'll get her settled and see you later." He walked after her slowly leaving us in silence at the table.

"He looks so sad," I said aloud after a few minutes.

"Did he know she was a bitch when he married her?" asked Rosalie. We all chuckled in response, but I wanted to know the answer to Rosalie's question. Could Catherine have changed so much through the course of their short marriage or was it Erik? It turns out… I didn't have to wait long to find out.

Sleep was evading me. Tossing and turning for over an hour, I decided a late-night walk would help. I loved listening to the bullfrogs croaking out their nightly chorus as I walked under an umbrella of stars. I turned and decided to walk along the darker path that was lit by the moon and small landscaping lights we had sprinkled around. I stopped and looked around at the dark silhouettes the lighting made. "It's just as beautiful at night," I said aloud.

"I agree," came a familiar voice. I turned around and smiled as Erik came into view. He had on the same clothes as earlier, but his face looked like it had weathered a storm. "What are you doing out here so late?" he asked softly.

"Couldn't sleep. How's *Princess* Catherine?" I couldn't help myself with the sarcasm.

"Kel, I'm so sorry about how she acted. She can be a real arse." He smiled but it didn't quite make it up to his eyes like it normally did.

"I agree, but I *can* be a little too nosy sometimes," I admitted. He chuckled and nudged my shoulder with his. "You didn't seem like yourself tonight," I sighed. I could not for the life of me imagine Erik married to that woman.

"I didn't feel like myself. Catherine and I got into an argument on the way here, and it was taking everything in me to reign in my temper. She didn't want to come out here, even though she knew this was the final straw for me." Erik started pacing between the flower beds and his breathing became labored. If he could get this riled up just talking about their argument, I couldn't imagine how angry he must have been at the time. "She was running late, as usual. It honestly felt like she was doing it on purpose. We finally made it to the ferry. I was texting Jake our status, when she grabbed the phone out of my hand and refused to give it back, even acting like she was going to throw it overboard."

"What the—?" My mouth fell open.

"Right? I had the same look on my face as you. Shock. What the fuck?" He stopped pacing and grabbed his head with both hands. "I think she was just looking for a reaction. Like she wanted me to blow up so she could cast the blame on *me* for our doomed marriage."

I stayed silent… the heaviness of the moment felt like a blanket over us. Finally, I asked, "Has she always acted like that?"

Erik took a moment to answer. "Not really. I mean… yes, sometimes, sure, but it seems constant now." He was quiet for a moment as he thought. "Yep, that's it. She's *constantly* in a bitchy mood," he threw up his hands. "I can't take it anymore."

"What creates her bad mood? Has she told you?" I asked.

"It's a combination of things. We don't have anything in common anymore… if we ever did." He sighed as he combed his hand through his hair again. "She had just moved here from New York when we met, and she seemed to enjoy all the outdoor activities that I love. Now I think it was just because it was new. She loves the city and really wants to move back to New York where she's happier."

A lump formed in my throat. Would Erik move to New York? He'd been our friend for only a year, but he had become so important to Jake… and me too. "Would you go too?" I asked softly.

Erik shook his head. "Fuck no. Me in New York with only the view of other buildings? I don't think so. Seattle is too far away from the Peninsula sometimes. Besides, it wasn't just that." He took a breath. "She wants kids. I've been upfront from the beginning that I didn't. She thought I would change my mind."

I let out the breath I was holding. He was staying. "That would be a difficult hurdle to get over."

"It was, but I've decided. I'll talk to her tomorrow… Well, later today." He let out a long breath. "It's best for both of us. I should have listened to my mum," he laughed. After seeing my puzzled expression, he went on, "We had a short engagement, so my mum didn't meet Catherine until she came the week before the wedding. To put it mildly, she wasn't a fan. She said that it didn't even seem like I could talk to her." He paused, smiling wistfully at the memory then continued. "Of course, in hindsight, she was completely right. I would say Catherine and I aren't even friends any longer. Sad, right?"

"Maybe a little… but you're changing your path now. Plus, now you know to always listen to your mother," I offered, making him laugh. "You have plenty of time to find someone you fit with. And there's no rush since you don't want kids. So now we know you need to find someone that is..." I started ticking off on my fingers, "Number one: Someone you can talk to. Number two: Someone that loves it here."

"So far that's you, and you're taken. I don't think Jake would share much more of you with me anyway," he sighed with a little chuckle.

"Yeah, sorry, no throuples," I laughed. "And if Jake dies of mysterious causes, *you're* my number one suspect," I teased. "And don't think that sexy accent is going to get you out of it either. I'm oblivious to your charms."

Erik laughed, "You love my charms. Too bad they won't help with Princess Catherine."

"See! It fits, right?" We both laughed. "Go screw her brains out this weekend… that'll be a good send off."

"Right… That hasn't happened for a while. I even asked her if she knew how babies were made since she always says no," he admitted. I was stunned. Catherine had this sexy, gorgeous man begging for sex and she said no?

"Does she have someone else?" I asked hesitantly.

"Not that she admitted, but it wouldn't surprise me. The fact that I don't care should tell me all that I need to know," he yawned.

"True. Now you need some sleep. I'll see you tomorrow. Everything will be alright, Erik," I said, giving him a tight hug.

He squeezed me back and kissed the top of my head. "You and Jake are some of my favorites."

We started walking in opposite directions when I turned around. "Oh, and Erik…" I said in a loud whisper, "just so you know…," I teased wanting to boost his confidence. "If I didn't love Jake so much, you could screw my brains out any time you wanted!" I smiled. "Good night!" His deep laughter echoed across the farm as I walked back towards the house.

Chapter 5

Present Day...

"They ended things that day," I explained to Sam. She and I were still lying on the lounge chairs enjoying our cocktails as it grew dark. "Erik showed up at our door that afternoon asking if he could stay in our spare room for the night. Catherine wanted to stay in the cabin but not with him. He drove her back to Seattle the next morning, and she moved to a hotel, then on to New York. Last time I stalked her on social media, she was married and already had a couple of kids. She looked happy," I smiled and shrugged. "Erik has stayed in the main house when he's here ever since."

"But he still rents cabins for the Assholes or whatever?" Sam asked.

"Yep, that way he can fit another client into his trip, which means more money for me since he includes meals with his guide package. Most of the time, he ends up being my sous chef," I chuckled. "A couple of weeks ago, he put cinnamon in my taco meat instead of cumin! I was able to save it, but it was so funny."

"Oh shit! Do you even hear yourself right now?" Sam said, sitting up in her chair with an impish grin. I shrugged in response. *What was she talking about?* "Ha ha... he put cumin instead of cinnamon... ha ha ha," she said in a shrill, sing-songy voice.

I still have no clue. "It was actually cinnamon instead of cumin–" I said slowly.

"I don't care about the damn spices, Kelly!" she shrieked, then lowered her voice again. "You are *into* him. Like *into, into* him. You don't just want to bang him," Sam declared.

Shit. I hated it when she was right. But how could I *not* be into him? He was sexy as hell, we always had fun together, and he seemed to love my farm as much as I did.

"So I'm into him. So what? A piece of ass is what I need, not a real relationship, and he fits the bill," I professed.

"What makes him perfect as a piece of ass but not a real relationship?" she asked.

"He's young and fun, and I bet he would rock my world in the bedroom," I gushed. "But he probably wouldn't want anything long-term with me anyway. I would be a steppingstone to him having a happy, fulfilling life. I'd just like to have fun with him while I can and get laid on a semi-regular basis."

"Who cares how old he is? He couldn't have a happy, fulfilling life with you?" Sam questioned.

"I've lived a fulfilling life already. I was married to a man I loved and raised two awesome kids. I wouldn't want Erik looking back wishing he had a family of his own," I sighed. "Plus, I want to have some fun myself, not just grab the first young, hot thing that comes across my sight line... Jesus! How did shit get this deep? Let's just leave it at 'friends with benefits', okay?"

"Okay... but let the record show that he divorced his wife because he didn't want kids... so your reasoning sounds flawed. Plus, you said he calls you "love" and shit," Sam smirked.

"Shut up... It's just something the English say," I hissed. "Erik started calling me that the night Jake told everyone his cancer was back. It's just a term of endearment," I added, taking another drink of my wine. "It was a tough one."

Elyse Rundell

Chapter 6

Two years ago...

"What's going on?" Erik muttered under his breath, setting his used plate in the sink as I was cleaning up after dinner. Jake and I had invited over a few of our closest friends, and Erik was suspicious of the intent since it wasn't one of his normal guide weekends.

"He'll tell y'all soon," I sighed, throwing the sponge I was using onto Erik's dirty plate.

"Shit. It's back, isn't it?" he whispered.

I nodded, dipping my head down and gripping the edge of the sink, pleading with myself to keep the tears from spilling over. I could not believe that I still had tears left to shed. Jake's cancer was back. He had beaten it last year, but it was already back again and worse than ever.

Erik leaned in closer. "When does chemo start?" I shrugged and turned my head away. I knew that if I saw his reaction, I would lose the tiny thread of control I was holding.

"Dammit. He's not going to fight it?" he hissed. All I could do was shake my head in response. I didn't blame Jake for deciding not to fight. The chemo treatments nearly killed him last time, and he said back then that he wouldn't go through that again. He wanted to spend his last days on his terms. Erik would understand eventually. He stopped mumbling expletives and placed his hand on mine. "How are *you*?"

What a loaded question. I could only shrug again in response, still not trusting my voice or my emotions. I was hoping Jake would make his announcement soon. Luckily, Erik seemed to be the only one that picked up on my melancholy mood, but that tiny thread of control was starting to unravel. Erik came to my rescue…

"Jake," Erik called across the room, "Was there something you needed to talk to us about? Or did you just invite us over for a brilliant meal?"

"Well, it was a great meal," said Jake with a sad smile, "But there *is* something, Erik. Could everyone sit down?"

Jake went on to explain to everyone that his cancer was back and aggressive, already spreading to his bones.

We had already talked to our kids and decided he wasn't going to fight it. Chemotherapy would only buy him around six months at the very most but at a tremendous cost to his physical and mental well-being. He was tired and ready to stop fighting. The room was silent except for the sound of sniffling as tears fell from every eye in the room. June stood up and wrapped her arms around Jake, shaking as the sobs racked her body. Everyone then stood and hugs were given all around. We spent the rest of the evening telling crazy stories about the farm, drinking, and Larry even got his guitar out for some impromptu karaoke.

It was nearly midnight when only Jake and Erik were left sitting together on the deck. I was getting ready for bed, and everyone else had gone home. I was on my way to tell the guys goodnight, but their conversation drifting through the open sliding door made me stop and listen...

"...not a week after the funeral or anything." Jake grumbled.

"It would be her decision. Why are we even talking about this now?" Erik grumbled back. "You still have some time." *Were they talking about me? What would be my decision?*

"Now's as good a time as any," Jake replied. "Besides, you're here now so why not make plans."

"You and your bloody plans... It's late and you're tired. We'll talk later..." I started taking a few steps back in case they came in, but the raw emotion in Erik's voice made me stop. "But Jake... you know I'll always look after her."

"I know you will. I do. I could not trust anyone more," Jake replied gruffly, failing to hold in his emotions. I quietly walked back to the bedroom, not wanting to intrude on their emotional moment. Jake had not had a ton of friends in his life, and I was so happy that Erik came into the picture when he did. I thought about questioning Jake about what I had overheard. My curiosity was piqued, but I decided that I would let them keep it between themselves. I'm sure I'll find out at some point. Still feeling wide awake, I grabbed a book from my nightstand and read until Jake came to bed.

I took a glance at the clock…. 2:22am. I'd been tossing and turning since Jake came to bed. He had taken enough edibles to take down a horse, so his snores were yet another reason why sleep eluded me. *Fuck it.* The night air, my Kindle, and a smoke were just what the doctor ordered. I had just taken my first drag when I heard the sliding door behind me.

"Busted," I said, holding up my hands. "Are you a cop? If you are, you have to tell me."

"You do know weed is legal in Washington, right?" Erik grabbed the vaporizer from my hand and took a hit. "How can someone be so silly yet so sexy all at the same time?" he teased and sat down in the chair next to me.

"*Years* of practice," I smiled. "You can't sleep either?"

Erik sighed and laid his head back against the chair. "Not at all. Tonight's been heavy."

"I do feel a little better now that you know. I wanted him to call you, but Jake wanted to tell you in person."

Erik only nodded and we both stayed silent as we listened to the nearby creek gurgling and bullfrogs croaking their loud song. I snagged the vape from Erik's hand and took another hit. "Speaking of sexy... you dating anyone worth mentioning? I need a distraction."

"No one of any significance." He snagged the vape back from my hand and took another drag. "Maybe a few that were fun for the night, but no one that I fancied enough to stick around." I chuckled in response. "*What?*" he grimaced.

I chuckled more, "Surely someone as hot as you can find *someone.*"

"True," he said, pretending to groom his eyebrows while he gave me a half smirk. "Though you forgot I'm also a prick that can't stand most people. Besides, all others pale in comparison to you," he teased.

"True... you being a prick part at least," I smiled.

A few more quiet moments passed. Erik placed his hand on my arm causing me to look up. His sad eyes, which were even darker than usual in the moonlight, caught me by surprise, "Are you really okay with his decision?"

I gave Erik a sympathetic smile. "That last chemo session nearly killed him, Erik. You know, you were there. I really don't think he has it in him to go through that again... both physically or mentally. Especially since it will only give him a little more time with us... and what kind of quality will that time be?" I took another long, deep drag and slowly exhaled. "He wants to feel as good as he can in his last days with us, so I'm jumping on board. When plans

47

change you have to pivot," I shrugged. "What else can I do?"

Erik reached for the vape and took his own long drag. "You're my favorite people."

"You've said that before," I teased.

"Well, I mean it," he sat up and turned to face me taking my hand. "I'm here if you need anything. Fuck, Kel. I'm here even if you *don't* need anything. Just know that." His sincerity showed on his face.

"I do know that," I said, squeezing his hand. "Thank you, Erik. And just so you know… I'm here for you too." He looked at me skeptically. "I mean it. You and Jake have gotten so close, it's going to be hard on you too."

"I guess we'll just have to be there for each other then, love," he offered.

"Deal," I smiled and let go of his hand to stifle my yawn. "I'll see you in the morning. Thanks for the chat."

"Goodnight," he murmured as I went back inside and crawled into bed with Jake, still sawing logs, having stolen all of the covers from my side. He was a fraction of the man he had been before his initial diagnosis. I decided to let him keep the covers and snuggled up to him instead. My conversation with Erik whirled around in my mind as I closed my eyes. It would be so weird for Erik to be here and Jake gone, but it gave me comfort knowing I would not lose them both.

Chapter 7

Present Day...

"What would be your decision? Did you ever find ou–out?" Sam stammered. We had decided to take our wine on a night tour of the farm.

"Haven't yet," I muttered. "I just hope Erik is sticking around here for himself and not just out of a sense of obligation to Jake." We stopped walking as I thought about that night. "You know? I'm actually mad at Jake about it. It's like he's strapped me to Erik without asking me and guilt tripped him to do it." I hiccupped and stumbled on a small rock in the path.

"I wouldn't say Jake guilt tripped him," Sam advised as I shrugged. "Erik seems *very* happy to be here. His business does well here, he has a great set up… *you're* here," she crooned.

"Listen, I know everything is good right now. We have fun together. We both benefit from our business arrangement," I rambled and flung my arm out to stop Sam from walking. "Hell, I'm pretty damn sure we're gonna have sex. Our chemistry is off the charts… It would be a shame for us *not* to," I laughed, fanned myself and took another slug of my wine. "We're just going to have fun. I want him to experience what else is out there… For fuck's sake, *I* want to experience what else is out there," Sam and I were both laughing by the time I got it out.

"Sounds like you want your cake, and you want to eat it too," Sam quirked an eyebrow as she slid me a side-eyed glance.

"I do love cake," I smirked.

"I believe I'm done with the cake sampling in my life," she hinted.

"You met someone!?" I rejoiced, throwing my hands up to the sky.

"No, stupid! Don't you think I would have told you by now if I had? I'm *ready* to meet someone, is all I'm saying," she professed and started walking again towards the house.

"You never know when lightning will strike," I winked, knowingly.

"Saturday?" she asked and held up her fist like she was going to punch me.

"You never know," I said slyly. "You might enjoy the cake so much you have to move up here."

"Maybe one day. The kids have graduated college and are off my dime, so I'm not saying no," she took a deep breath. "It would just take some extra good cake."

Sam and I walked into the entrance of the main house. We passed one of Erik's flyers that was on a display rack for guests. His guide service logo was blazoned across the front along with all of the types of services he offered.

"Erik seems to love it up here as much as you do," she said with a comforting sigh. I nodded in agreement.

"He does. He loved Jake too. I swear he misses him as much as I do. He even tried to comfort me after Jake's funeral, but I'm not sure who comforted who more."

Elyse Rundell

Chapter 8

One year ago...

Life goes on... Jake's funeral had been a few weeks back. My kids had returned to their lives, saddened by the loss of their father, but hopeful for my newfound independence. Friends and family had returned to their respective homes, and Larry and I were left to master our new routine. My mood did seem marginally better today, but I gave the credit to Erik who was coming this evening instead of tomorrow for his guide weekend. It would be good to see him and catch up, but a little apprehension bubbled at the surface. It would be Erik's first visit since Jake passed, and I hoped we could have some semblance of normalcy and not be blubbering messes all weekend.

I was leaning against the front porch post when Erik pulled into the drive that evening. All my chores were done, and my pipe was packed, just waiting on company. My eyes brimmed with tears as soon as I saw his face through the windshield, he looked older with shadows underneath his eyes like he hadn't slept… he looked sad. I shrugged off the post and walked to him as he got out of his SUV, wrapping my arms around him and squeezed as he sobbed into my shoulder.

"God, I'm sorry, Kel, I'm just gutted," Erik said after a few minutes as we dried our tears. "And I thought I was coming to cheer *you* up."

Ten minutes later we were sitting comfortably on the back deck, passing my cannabis pipe back and forth enjoying the mellowing effects.

"Thanks again for the flowers. They really brighten up the room," I glanced back at the cheery bouquet on the center of my kitchen island through the glass door.

"I saw a woman carrying them today when I was out on my run," Erik said, shrugging, "I thought you'd like them, so I ran up to Pike's Market and got them for you."

"Well, that was awfully nice of you," I smiled. "Who knew you could be so thoughtful?" I teased.

Erik laughed, "I'm not *always* an arsehole."

"Not always," I smiled. "Sunflowers *are* my favorite."

"I know," he said and laid his head back on the lounge chair to look at the stars. We sat in silence listening to the creek rushing over the rocks.

"How are you holding up… really?" I asked, looking out into the blackness of the forest beyond.

Erik let out a sarcastic bark of laughter. "I don't think I can be the bloke that complains about his best friend dying to his bloody widow."

I glanced over and gave him a tender smile. "If not me, then who? Wouldn't I understand better than anyone?" I asked honestly.

He studied me intently before replying, "You may have a point."

"I usually do," I smiled.

"It's just that I'll think of something and want to get his opinion on it, and it'll hit me that he's not there to give me an answer," he sighed. "Then, it's like a wave of sadness hits me and it's hard to set myself back on track."

"I completely get it. The same exact thing happens to me, but I'm hoping that wave will get smaller and smaller, though probably not ever go away entirely. We'll learn how to exist with it, and it will get easier. It has to," I sighed. "At least that's how it's been for me in the past. I lost my dad when I was young and then my mother a while back from Alzheimer's. I assume it will be the same when losing my husband, just that much harder."

"I meant what I said last year. I'm here for you, even when you don't need anything," he replied quietly.

"And I meant it when I said we needed to be there for each other. We're off to a good start so far," I smiled.

"I agree," said Erik.

"I mean, you're already telling me I'm right… you've learned the most important lesson," I slid him a grin with a mischievous wink. He laughed aloud as I launched into a string of stories of times when Jake should have listened to me. He added his own of when he should have listened to Jake that had us both laughing out loud.

"So, the logical conclusion," I said trying to stifle my laughter, "with Jake gone, both you and Larry just need to listen to me from now on."

"Haven't we always?" Erik asked, making me laugh again. "Careful with my mate, Larry. Rosalie might think she has competition."

My whole body shook with laughter. "I *love* Larry… I do. I could not do this without him, *but* I think I just threw up in my mouth a little bit." We decided that was a good way to end the night and made plans to do it again Saturday, once Erik got back from his guide trip.

I had just taken a batch of blackberry muffins from the oven when Erik walked in on Saturday, sweaty and dirty from his trip. Larry picked up he and his group of Assholes at one of the distant trailheads since they had been gone for two full days. I was looking forward to hanging out with Erik again. The night that he and I had spent on the deck was the first night that I hadn't cried myself to sleep in ages. It seemed that a little positivity had crept back into my life, and I had hoped that Erik felt the same.

"Hey! Welcome back!" I smiled and started taking the muffins out of the pan.

"Thanks... muffins at eight o'clock at night?" he asked.

"Breakfast tomorrow for your Assholes," I smiled. "How was the ride?"

"Really good. It felt good to get back out there." His eyes kept wandering down to my muffins. "I'll be your best friend if you let me have one of those."

"Uh... you already are my best friend," I teased, "but yes you can have my muffin." I smiled wondering if he would pick up on my funny innuendo. I handed him a glass of water as he shoved the muffin in his mouth.

"Your muffin tastes great," he said with a mouthful of muffin and an impish grin. *I knew he'd get it.*

"That's what I've been told," I smirked, grabbing a drink of my own water since my throat was suddenly dry.

"We are talking about your pussy, right?" Erik asked innocently.

Water sprayed all across the kitchen island as I started choking from laughing. A small little coughing fit and I was finally able to talk. "Please wait until I swallow before you say funny shit," I choked out.

"I'm not even touching that one...," he said walking back with his hands up in surrender. I laughed and flipped him off. Erik ran up to shower and change while I finished cleaning the kitchen. It felt great to joke around like we always had and have that semblance of normalcy.

I was sitting on the deck, cocktail in hand, when Erik came back down.

"I wasn't sure if you wanted a cocktail, smoke, or sobriety," I called from my seat.

"What are you having?"

"Whiskey and coke."

He walked out a few minutes later with two whiskey and cokes and handed one to me.

"Let's get drunk," he smiled as he clinked my glass with his.

"You don't have to twist my arm," I teased.

Erik filled me in on his trip and showed some of the pictures he took along the way. He seemed more like himself today, so getting back on his bike must have been good for him. Larry and Rosalie joined us for drinks and entertainment. Entertainment being them bickering back and forth over just about everything. It was good-natured, usually, but I always found them hilarious. They only stuck around for one drink before heading off to bed mumbling something about "you youngsters."

"Funny considering Rosalie is younger than me," I admitted, "but I have always been a little immature."

"I'd say more young-at-heart," Erik offered. He sounded like he was going to say something else then stopped himself. I stayed quiet, letting him think about whatever it was he wanted to say. "Our hang out the other night was good for me. I hope it was good for you too," he said shyly. I didn't think I had ever heard him sound so unsure of himself. I was humbled.

"Oh, Erik. It was good for me too. I feel a little more positive and not quite alone through all this. Thanks for that. I truly mean it," I comforted. He smiled with relief.

"Now… let's dish, tell me more about Larry and Rosalie," he said flamboyantly, crossing his legs. I filled Erik in on the soap opera cycle that was Larry's relationship. He had heard a lot of it before from Jake, but it had been a while since he'd had an update.

"They're in their sweet spot right now, so they should be good for a while... barring anything out of the ordinary. They do entertain me." I smiled contentedly.

"They *are* entertaining," he beamed, "I see why you keep them around."

We stayed up late swapping stories of other colorful people in our past that have entertained us, until we were both yawning more than speaking. Plans were made for another hangout in a couple of weeks, and we called it a night. My cheeks were sore from laughing as I turned the light out and closed my eyes. *What a nice weekend.*

Elyse Rundell

Chapter 9

Present Day...

"We've really been there for each other this past year," I smiled.

"Sounds like y'all really did help each other find some normalcy then," Sam yawned as I turned the lights off in the kitchen. It was late and my alarm was set to go off early in the morning.

"Things *were* normal until about three months ago... but I'll tell you that over breakfast. It's too late tonight," I yawned as well. "Cheese popovers for breakfast in the morning."

"I won't argue about that. Good night!" Sam called as she headed upstairs.

"Goodnight!" I said loudly. I went to bed with visions of dark-brown, smirking eyes eating cheese popovers and blackberry muffins in my dreams.

I had already put away breakfast for my cabin guests in the lobby when Sam came stomping downstairs. She was not a morning person and needed caffeine and sustenance before she could function. Knowing this about her, I had coffee and hot, cheesy popovers waiting for her when she sat at the kitchen island. I could see her mood brighten immediately.

"I love you," she mumbled as she stuffed half of the buttery popover in her mouth and moaned. "Are you sure you're not a lesbian?"

I laughed, "Strictly dickly... is that how it goes?" Shrugging, I offered another clue about her potential love interest to wake her up, "But I hear your new friend that is coming over tomorrow night can hold her own in the kitchen."

"I really do love you," Sam grinned. "Where did we leave off last night?" She was already reaching for another popover. Luckily, I had one last batch in the oven. I thought back to last night through the wine haze.

"Three months ago... Erik and my relationship was somewhat back to normal until about three months ago," I remembered, thinking back to that weekend. "It was when

Lindsey was here for a long weekend, and Erik found out I was thinkin' about dating."

"Lindsey. College-roommate Lindsey?" I nodded in response as I took the popovers out of the oven. "Hold up! Dating? What happened?" Sam mumbled as she stuffed another popover in her mouth.

Elyse Rundell

Chapter 10

Three months ago…

"I know it's a short trip, but I'm so happy that you came," I beamed at Lindsey as we sipped our margaritas and watched the sunset. She had flown in that morning for a long weekend trip, and we had spent the entire time catching up. Today was the first time we'd seen each other since Jake's funeral.

"I'm happy I came too. I needed it as much as you did," she sighed, looked out at the sunset and took a deep breath. "Is it bad that I'm a little jealous of your situation?"

I gave her a look of confusion. "Jealous of my situation? What do you mean?"

She gave a bit of a maniacal laugh and shook her head. "Sorry, it must be the margaritas going to my head. Nevermind, I'm talking nonsense," she resigned.

"Linds, talk to me. Are you okay?" I touched her arm as I sat forward. "You can talk to me about anything." She sighed again, and I could tell she was gathering her thoughts.

"I thought things would be different now, with Rick and me. You know? With the kids being out of the house… it's our time to do the things that we want to do together. Like we talked about when they were younger. Now…" She shrugged and took a sip of her margarita. "Now… It's like, he wants to do his thing and I'm happy because that means I get to do whatever I want. I know it's terrible to say… and I'd only ever say this to you, but it would almost be easier if he died. Crap, I'm going to hell, right?" she cried and took another larger sip of her drink. I took a rather large sip of mine to buy me some time to respond.

"Well, no… I don't think you're going to hell, not unless you actually kill him," I smiled. "You do know there's this thing called a divorce. I hear that it really works well for some people."

She rolled her eyes and took another large drink. "I know that's always an option, but what would I tell people when they ask why we split? We're not *friends* anymore? I'd feel like an asshole." She shook her head and took another drink. "Maybe he'll cheat on me! Do you think?

Then BOOM… divorce time, baby!" I laughed since it was obvious the margaritas were kicking in.

"Easy there, Jose Cuervo. Eat something," I chuckled and pushed the tray of munchies towards her. She laughed, raised her glass, then reached for the chips and guacamole. I continued, "First and foremost, don't worry about what anyone else thinks. This is *your* life and the only one you're likely to get. Decide what *you* want, then go from there." I shook my head and chuckled, "Do you really think Rick would cheat on you?"

"Probably not, but I wouldn't cry if he did," she smiled. "What about you? Anyone interesting on the horizon?"

"Me? Maybe…" I shrugged and gave an innocent grin. "Okay, there's this guy named Ray who owns a local lavender farm that I've been flirting with at different town events. He's cute and super nice… I'm not going to ask *him* out, but I'll go if he asks me."

"How exciting!" Lindsey squealed and clapped her hands.

I took another long pull from my margarita. "Exciting is not the term I would use to describe him, but we've had good conversation so far," I smiled.

"That's always a good start. Speaking of excitement, when is Jake's hot, guide friend getting here? We need some eye candy!" Lindsey exclaimed.

"His name is Erik," I giggled, shaking my head. "Larry left with the transport van a few hours ago, so they should be back any time now."

"Does he still stay with you a lot? The hot friend?" she asked in a conspiratorial whisper, pouring herself another margarita from the pitcher then topped mine off.

"Erik. Yes. Every other weekend. He's been great. He even brought me those flowers, but he does that all the time." I motioned to the beautiful bouquet that was in the window. "He and I usually sit out here and talk all night about damn near everything when he's here. Between Erik and ol' Larry, I can't complain about being lonely. For sure." I looked up and Lindsey was eyeing me suspiciously.

"Careful with that young'un, girl. You sound like you like him," she teased, causing me to laugh loudly.

"You've seen him, right? Who *wouldn't* like him? He's sexy as *hell*," I shouted the last word cupping my hands around my mouth making Lindsey whoop with laughter.

"Who might that be?" came a deliciously wicked, English accent through the open sliding door. *Holy shit.*

My widened eyes flew to Lindsey's which mirrored my own. We both broke into loud, raucous laughter that must have drawn Erik's interest further, since he joined us on the deck. *I need a driveway alarm.* Lindsey and I both reached for our drinks as I tried to think of a witty comeback, but I was too distracted by our new view. Erik was clad in his black spandex biking outfit that hugged his body like a second skin. I had fantasies about taking those shorts off of him, but those were between myself and my vibrator.

"Eyes up here, ladies," Erik scolded playfully. I guess Lindsey must have been enjoying the new view as well.

"You'll need to go change before you have a drink with us," I chuckled. "The drunker we get, the hornier we get."

"I can tell," he grinned, "Be back in a jif." He turned and jogged back inside.

My eyes met Lindsey's as we both said in mock English accents, "Be back in a jif," and rolled with laughter. A loudly accented "shut up" through the window made Lindsey go running for the toilet in fear of her full bladder. I was still chuckling when Erik sauntered back out surprisingly quickly, changed, and twirling the stem of an empty margarita glass between his fingers. He had beaten Lindsey out, so I hoped her full bladder didn't win. Erik took a seat at the other end of the couch that I was on and handed me his empty glass.

"Filler up... sounds like I need to catch up. Lindsey in the loo?" he asked, draping his arm along the back of the couch towards me and crossing his ankle over his knee. He looked so relaxed... and delicious. *What? Easy there, ol' girl. It's just the margaritas talking.*

"Are you singing?" I giggled. "*Filler up, catch up, Lindsey in the loo,*" I sang while my arms flung about like I was conducting an orchestra.

Erik laughed and shook his head while I filled up his glass to the brim. "We should have margaritas more often," he teased and gave me his sinful smirk, making my breath hitch. *Damn margaritas.* Lindsey rejoined us and I was happy to see that she had on her same pants.

69

Conversation flowed smoothly after that with Erik telling us about his trip and Lindsey filling us in on life in Texas, notably leaving out talk of her marriage. I spoke of future plans for the farm and margaritas flowed while the sunlight around us disappeared.

"So, when do you think this local guy is going to ask you out?" asked Lindsey between bites of chips and salsa. Cringing, I glanced toward Erik, but he seemed to be preoccupied with the margarita in his hand. *Not that I care what he thinks.*

"Any time now… though I'm rusty with the whole dating process," I shrugged.

"You're dating?" questioned Erik. I couldn't quite place what the emotion was on his face, but it didn't seem good.

"I haven't *yet,* but I'm open to the idea." My eyes narrowed as I watched him, the tequila loosening my mouth filter. "Is that going to be a problem?"

"Should it be a problem?" he replied, not wavering his stare. I guess it loosened his filter too. I had lost track of where we were in this dating conversation. He took a breath, "I thought you would have told me, that's all."

"I'm telling you now," I smiled. Erik smiled but it didn't quite reach his somber-filled eyes. I'm sure it would be weird to see me with someone that wasn't his best friend.

"Y'all are killing my buzz with all this dating talk!" Lindsey yelped, jumping up from her seat.

"You're the one that brought it up!" I replied loudly. "Here, I'll put on some music so we can dance." A few taps on my phone and an old George Strait song drifted through the air from the outdoor speakers.

"Yes! Leave it there. I have to use the bathroom again," she laughed as she flitted away. *Bathroom again?*

"No more dating talk," I taunted Erik in a faux tone of authority, then started humming along to the familiar chorus of the song that had started. "Wanna dance, cowboy?"

"I don't know how to dance to this rubbish," he chuckled but stood up. I jumped to my feet and opened my arms in invitation.

"I'll teach you…," I grinned mischievously. Erik looked up to the sky and shrugged his arms.

"Why not, you little vixen," he murmured and took a step closer.

"Yay! Okay… you put your hand up here, and I'll put my hand here, okay. Now we'll hold hands like this." I helped place his hands in the proper positions. "Got it. Now, you'll lead and I'll follow," I said, looking up at him and smiling.

"I'll believe that when I see it," Jake mumbled, then flashed me his sexiest smirk. Being so close, I could almost see a twinkle in his eye.

"Shut it. Now we'll go forward two steps then back one, then forward two back one… with the music," I advised. He kept that same damn smirk on his stupid, sexy face.

Erik picked up on the two-step quickly, and we danced around the deck dodging chairs and potted plants, laughing when I missed a step instead of him.

"The teacher has become the master," he laughed, bowing to me when the song was over as I rolled my eyes. An old Bellamy Brothers song came on that made my rolling eyes widen with delight. "Want to –," he began.

"YES!" I yelped before Erik could even finish his question. We danced around the deck with only a couple of issues that time, and he even added a twirl at the end. He pulled me close and I laid my head on his chest as the next song started. We swayed as the country singer crooned about drinking too much and losing his love.

"I think I might be good at this," he teased softly.

"I think so," I murmured, closing my eyes. I took a deep breath and enjoyed the moment, the cool night air, dulled senses from the margaritas, being held in Erik's strong arms. *Damn margaritas.*

"Who were you talking about when I got here earlier?" he asked. *Shit.*

"I don't remember," I mumbled and tried to duck my head lower.

"Woo!" he teased, "Were you talking about me, love? Did you say that I was um, let me see... How did it go? Um... 'sexy as hell'?" he grinned, tipping my chin up to look him in the eye.

"What? You? No way," I lied, feeling flushed. *Damn margaritas.* "I was talking about Larry... Oh yeah, that Larry is sexy as *hell!*" I laughed as I kept his stare, but I was sure he could hear my heart pounding. Glancing down at his mouth, I wondered for the hundredth time what his lips would feel like.

"Coward," Erik murmured just as a loud rumbling came from the kitchen.

"It's hot tub time!" shrieked Lindsey as she ran out of the house in her swimsuit. I wondered where she had been for so long. Erik and I both instinctively took a step away from each other. "Y'all go get your suits on… or don't," she laughed, winking at Erik. Lindsey rolled into the tub causing a big wave to splash over the side.

"I will if you will," I grinned at Erik.

"I don't know…," he started.

"Coward," I smirked, trying my best to imitate him.

"I *will*," he challenged, looking me squarely in the eye. Erik took off his shirt and threw it on the table, earning a look of confusion from me. He unbuttoned his pants and yelled, "Last one in has to sit on my lap!" *Sit where?*

I gasped as he dropped his pants and ran over to the hot tub, jumping in wearing only his boxer briefs and a grin. Lindsey was in hysterics as the water bobbed all around her, not caring that her whole head was soaked. For a split second, I considered skinny dipping just for shock value, but good sense won out and I was back in record time wearing my favorite swimsuit. It had a built-in bustier that made my tits look fantastic.

I wasn't sure if it was the temperature of the water, the tequila, or being so close to Erik, but the water was uncomfortably warm when I slid in. I didn't bring up his proposed seating arrangement, but I wasn't sure how long I was going to be able to stay in the hot water. I stood up and sat on the edge of the tub with my legs in the water to even out my temperature. The night air that hit my heated skin was a cooling blanket that felt exquisite.

"Where are you going?" asked Erik with concern. He was probably afraid Lindsey might jump his bones if they were alone.

"Nowhere, it's just too hot to be all the way in," I moaned, feeling flushed.

"You can't take the heat?" he taunted, giving me the full wattage of his sexy smirk.

"I guess not," I smiled.

"Me either," said Lindsey flopping onto my lap and closing her eyes. I smiled thoughtfully and placed my hand on her shoulder to make sure she didn't fall asleep. I looked up at Erik who had the strangest look on his face as he stared at me, concentrating, like I was a puzzle to be solved. My swimsuit was working overtime with my boobs pushed up looking like a whore in a brothel. *Aw hell, Kelly, you're putting it all out there.* I roused Lindsey and we all got out and dried off with the towels I remembered to grab.

"I hate to be a party pooper," Lindsey whined once we were settled back in our original places, "but I think I might call it a night."

"What? So early?" I asked, though a glance at the clock showed me it wasn't early at all.

"These margaritas have done me in. We should have made tacos before we started drin–king," she hiccupped at the end and started to go inside.

"True… so, so true," I agreed. "Breakfast tacos in the morning," I yelled, but she had already gone. "Hey, you," I said, poking Erik with my foot as he remained at the other end of the couch. "Are you going to leave me too?"

Picking up my foot, Erik held it with both his hands. Slowly he started to massage deep in the arch of my foot, making me moan, he knew without asking where I liked it. "I could never leave you," he mumbled, staring down at my foot. He answered my question, but I got the impression he had more than one meaning.

"Because Jake told you not to?" I asked quietly. Erik stopped the massage and looked up at me with confusion in his eyes. "I heard you and Jake talking that night on the deck after he told everyone the cancer was back. I know he told you to watch out for me, but I'm okay... don't feel like you *have* to be here." Tears welled in my eyes, but I refused to let them spill over. "I don't want to stand in the way of you living your life, because you feel obligated to Jake." *Damn margaritas.*

Erik picked both of my feet up and scooted closer to me on the couch laying my legs across his lap. The only way to be closer was if I were actually sitting in his lap, as he placed his hand on my cheek and I leaned into his touch. The look of tenderness in his eyes pierced my soul, and I knew I would never forget this moment no matter how much tequila I had.

"I'm here because I *want* to be here, Kelly. There's no place else I'd rather be," I could see the sincerity in his eyes as he stroked my cheek. "You're not standing in my way... you're walking this journey with me." His hand was so warm against my skin. I closed my eyes and smiled dreamily.

"Sure, I'm fun to hang out with... but I don't want you to ever look back and regret that you missed out on anything, especially because of me." I whispered, opening my eyes.

"What could I possibly regret?" he asked, with a soul-crushing look in his deep, brown eyes.

I threw my arms in the air. "Not having a family, not having a fulfilling fucking life. I already had all those things, and I feel like I would be taking your chances away for that if you were too wrapped up hanging out with me." I crossed my arms over my chest for emphasis... *Or maybe just to keep them to myself.*

"What makes a fucking life fulfilling is not the same for everyone, Kelly." He sighed then was quiet again. What I would give to know what was going through his mind. He said quietly, still looking into the dark night, "I wish you would have told me you were ready."

"Ready? What am I ready for?" I asked.

"I don't know... To move on? A relationship? Or just something more?" He sat up and turned around, looking me squarely in the eye.

"I'm *not* ready for a relationship... not a full-time one at least. I like having my independence and not having to check-in with anyone." I took a deep breath. "I had a happy marriage with Jake. I'm not looking to duplicate that..." I closed my eyes to avoid his stare. "You know what I'd like, Erik? You know what I'm *ready* for? A friend. A really great friend. With benefits. With really great benefits. That's what I'm ready for," I breathed and opened my eyes. Erik's gaze was laser focused on my lips taking in every word. "Someone that sees me not just as a widow or mother, someone that I can have fun with, someone that... someone that... will fuck the shit out of me."

Erik's head jerked up, his eyes meeting mine, then crinkled with the smirk I knew so well. "I hope you do mean figuratively."

I shrugged and smiled. "Figuratively. Now that's enough soul searching for tonight." I yawned and closed my eyes, "I'm going to bed." Erik seemed closer when I opened my eyes, uncomfortably closer. I must have leaned in when I closed my eyes. My eyes widened in surprise. "It's getting late, and I– I– drank too much," I stammered. I leaned back, swung my legs off Erik and stood up rather quickly, too quickly. I swayed, feeling dizzy, as Erik stood up and grabbed my shoulders to steady me.

"I'll walk you in," he soothed, steering me inside by placing his arm around my shoulder. I didn't realize just how woozy I was until I started walking. Erik walked me into my bedroom where I fell onto the bed, grateful for the soft surface. I felt him remove my flip flops, and heard him mumbling, but I couldn't quite make sense of what he was saying. *Damn margaritas.*

"Don't go…" I whined, reaching out for him since I was too dizzy to open my eyes. He held my hand, and I felt the bed dip from his weight as he sat down. "Just stay with me… for a little while." I heard him mumbling but could not understand. Then, the bed moved as he crawled over and cuddled next to me, still holding my hand. I turned to my side as he spooned me closer. I brought his hand to my lips and kissed the back of it. "Thank you," I whispered.

"Good night, vixen," he murmured so close to my ear I could feel the warmth from his breath.

"I like that," I whispered, giggling softly as I snuggled against him. I could feel that the room was no longer spinning, but I kept my eyes closed since sleep threatened.

"What do you like?" Erik murmured even closer to my ear, so close I could almost feel his lips touch my earlobe.

"Vix-en," I growled softly. I wished I could open my eyes, but they were too heavy from tequila and sleep.

"Does it make you feel naughty?" His voice sounded raspy now, still low and close to my ear.

"Uh-huh," I confirmed as best I could.

"Do you like when I make you feel naughty?" he whispered with that same raspy voice.

I do. The last thought before I drifted into a drunken slumber, not sure if I said it aloud or not.

The sun woke me the next morning, shining its bright light right on my face. I stirred but something heavy lying across me was making it hard to move. I barely opened my eyes to see half of Erik's body slung over me still asleep. I screwed my eyes shut again and tried to replay my memories of last night. I did feel a shift in our relationship, a few times actually, but I wasn't going to jump to conclusions after one tequila-fueled, emotional night.

Erik started to move and stretch his body on top of me as he began to wake. I kept my eyes closed and mimicked his movements pretending I was waking up as well, when something hard jutted against my hip making my eyes fly open in surprise.

"Shit! Sorry," Erik laughed, adjusting himself, his dark hair a mess and swept over one eye. "Little Erik has a mind of his own in the morning," he laughed, his voice groggy from sleep. I could not control the loud laughter that burst from my throat.

"Did–" I tried, "Did *you* just call your *dick...* LITTLE ERIK?" I shouted the name to the ceiling as another fit of laughter came over me. This may have been the funniest thing I've heard all year. I finally laid my head back down on my pillow and took a deep breath, but another chuckle bubbled up.

"Let me get this straight." Erik blasted me with his sexist smirk as he propped his head on his hand next to me. "I've just jabbed you with my erect penis after spending the night in your bed, and you're *laughing* at me. Am I correct?"

"I was laughing *with* you," I smiled then erupted into laughter again. He really did laugh then and laid his head back on the pillow.

"You really must be my favorite person for me to endure all this abuse," he said dramatically as he brought his hand up to his forehead, feigning dismay. I got up, still wearing my swimsuit from the night before, and threw my pillow which landed perfectly on his head.

"Would breakfast tacos help?" I asked.

"I don't have time. I've got to get a couple of the guys back this morning. I'll grab a shower then go." I saw a look of disappointment cross his face before he rolled out of bed and grabbed his shoes off the floor.

I had 'to-go' coffees waiting for him and his two Assholes when Erik came back down, after packing up his things, along with a box of homemade pastries that I knew he loved.

"*This* is why I endure the abuse," he laughed as he perused his box of goodies. "I love any chance I get to munch your muffin," he taunted.

I rolled my eyes as I sipped my coffee. "It's actually a pastry," I stated matter-of-factly.

"I love any chance I get to pound your pastry," he looked me squarely in the eye and took a sip of his coffee. His straight face turned into a smile when I laughed. "Thank you for the dance lessons last night."

"You're welcome. You were a fast learner," I admitted. "We'll have to do it again sometime."

"We will," he agreed. It was already past the time Erik had said he needed to leave, but it seemed like he was stalling when it came to walking out the door. "Are you really going to go out with that bloke Lindsey was discussing?"

I was not expecting that question. "If he asks," I shrugged.

"So, you'll go on a bloody date with this wanker, fall in love and get married. Is that how this works?" he snapped. *What in the actual hell?*

I looked at Erik like he was crazy. "I have no idea how this works, but you seem to have it all figured out," I fumed. *Where was this attitude coming from?* "I highly doubt I'll go on one date with this guy and fall in fucking love, *besides* I don't want to get married again… as if it's any of your fucking business!" I did not remember a recent time that I had been this angry, and never at Erik. I stood there and stared at him, my eyes wide, waiting for his response.

Erik met my stare for a good minute before finally lowering his gaze and shaking his head. "Sorry," he sighed, and took a deep breath. "It's like I saw your life all lined up for you, and I didn't see where I would fit," he lamented then raised his eyes to mine, his brown eyes revealing the hurt he must have felt.

"Like I said last night," I breathed, "a friend with benefits is all I want… a distraction from my grief or life, whatever. We're not going to have to worry about where *you'll* fit in because you always will, so drop it… please," I added and touched his chin. I didn't trust myself to touch him anywhere else. "Now go," I smiled and pushed him toward the door. "I'll see you in a couple of weeks… No! Wait! I'll be in Mexico with my family that weekend, then Texas after that for the holidays. Who knows when you'll get to see me next?"

"I'll be in England the following month visiting *my* family," he sighed and wrapped his arms around me in a huge, bear hug. "Who knows when you'll get to see *me* next?"

"Bye, weird-o," I grumbled into his shoulder. He kissed me on top of my head and squeezed one last time.

"Bye, *vixen*," he growled in my ear then kissed my neck. He winked as he turned around with a flourish, grabbed his things and walked out the door without looking back. *Holy fuck.*

Elyse Rundell

Chapter 11

Present Day...

"We didn't see each other again until two weeks ago," I sighed to Sam as I grabbed vegetables from the fridge to start meal prep for dinner service. Erik and his Assholes would arrive this evening, and he had texted to say they would eat here at the big house. Sam was a convenient guest to have any time, since she preferred to stay around the farm, relax, and watch me work.

"Dancing, sexy stares, *and* he slept with you? And who is this local guy you're interested in? You haven't mentioned him at all!" Sam's mouth hung open in shock. Larry's voice blared from the walkie talkie that was sitting on the kitchen counter.

"Kelly? You there? I need your help in the barn. Bring your gloves!" I held a finger up to Sam to pause as I replied to Larry.

"On my way, *shit!* Sorry, Larry, I dropped my squash." I didn't want him to think it was because I had to go help him. I bent down to grab the culprit that had rolled under the cabinet.

"Shit is right. I need your help shoveling it!" he laughed in reply.

"That's because you're full of it!" I howled.

"Tell Sam to get her lesbian ass out here too. I need something pretty to look at with strong hands," he replied. Being politically correct was not exactly in Larry's wheelhouse, but we were working on it.

"Fuck you. I'll be there in a minute," I laughed into the walkie as Sam rolled her eyes. "I'll finish the story later. You can stay here if you want," I said to Sam. Larry could ogle her some other time.

"It's fine. I'll put a baggy sweatshirt on for Larry's benefit. Try and crush his spirit," she laughed.

"Hell, good luck, he'd love that too!" We laughed and headed out to the barn.

Hours later, Sam and I were lounging on the back deck having helped Larry in the barn (he said he would use his imagination due to Sam's outerwear), arranged a dinner spread for Erik and his Assholes on the kitchen island and gotten comfortable. My chores were done, drinks were flowing, and we were kicked back on my favorite deck loungers, waiting for the evening's activities to commence.

"It's so relaxing here," Sam sighed as we looked out at the surrounding forest. "Quiet and peaceful," she breathed in and sighed. "Ready to tell me about the local guy?"

"Thanks, it's my happy place," I sighed in return. "The local guy is named Ray. I wish there was more to tell, but he's pretty–," My phone chimed alerting me that there was movement at the front door. "Erik's here! Remember, play it cool," I hissed at Sam, feeling like there was a knot in my stomach.

"As cool as a cucumber," Sam slurred, raising her glass in my direction.

I rolled my eyes just as Erik stepped through the sliding door smiling at my expression, "Isn't it a little early for eye rolling, love?" he asked with a grin.

"It's never too early for eye rolling," I laughed as he leaned down to hug me in greeting. *God, he looked good.* His snug, white T-shirt was my favorite thing he wore, and he usually paired it with a flannel shirt like tonight. He hugged me tight, and I felt the muscles in his body tense when he squeezed. "Erik, this is Sam... Sam, this is Erik. It's hard to believe that the two of you haven't met before." Sam had been sick when we had Jake's funeral and had been unable to attend.

"The infamous Erik, so nice to finally meet you," smiled Sam in greeting.

"The equally infamous Sam. I hear you know where the bodies are buried," Erik replied while cocking a dark eyebrow.

"Only the ones I helped bury," said Sam as she took a sip of her drink. We all laughed as Erik picked up my legs from the lounge chair and sat down, placing my legs back on his lap, squeezing my socked feet. I saw Sam raise an eyebrow in my peripheral vision.

"Did you have dinner plans for us? I'm starving!" Erik asked while at the same time his stomach let out a rumble.

"Uh… it's out on the kitchen island. Did I need to fix you a plate and feed you too?" I teased. *How could he have missed the spread we had laid out?*

"That could be fun," he grinned, dumping my legs from his lap, "but I don't have time for fantasies." He jumped up quickly from the lounger and went back inside. I whipped my head around to Sam and shrugged my shoulders. "Holy shit!" he yelled. "How did I miss all this?"

"That's what I was wondering!" I yelled back.

"I guess I was just too eager to find *you*," he said, poking his head out the door.

"Find me for what?" I asked, meeting his gaze. Just a few seconds passed before he spoke, but it felt like an eternity.

"To say hello, silly woman," Erik smirked and pulled his head back inside. I looked at Sam again and this time it was her turn to shrug. Minutes later, Erik returned with a heaping plate of food and resumed his seat at the end of my chair this time without my feet in the way.

"I guess you *are* hungry," I commented, glancing down at the full plate. "Will the Assholes need food tonight or should I wrap it up for tomorrow?"

"I'll check," he said, chuckling at the familiar nickname. Erik grabbed his phone and began texting and received a reply right away. "Bloody hell. They really are arseholes. They want it in their cabins," he grumbled. The Assholes were earning their nickname today. I started to get up, but Erik put his hand on my leg. "I'll go, you stay with your mate and relax. Be back in a jif,"

"Oooo thank you-oo-oo... that's why I keep you around," I sang as he got up and went inside grumbling under his breath about inconsiderate assholes.

"I like him," Sam said in a hushed voice. "Tell me what happened a couple of weeks ago."

I got up and closed the sliding glass door to make sure we couldn't be overheard. Erik was talking to one of the Assholes on speaker phone while he packed up the food but looked up with a smile when he heard the door closing. I returned his smile with a wink and came back to my lounge chair.

"Alright, two weeks ago..."

Elyse Rundell

Chapter 12

Two weeks ago...

Thursday evenings were normally a busy time for me, but I had made an exception that night. I was going to get *laid*. Ray the Local and I had gone out a few times over the last couple of months with a couple of semi-memorable makeout sessions under our belt. I was ready to knock one out of the park. I thought it would also help with a different problem. *Erik.* Our paths had not crossed in nearly three months, since the night we had slept together. We had both been traveling so it wasn't that we did it on purpose, but he would be here tomorrow. I was so horned up that I knew I needed to get laid before he got here, then maybe I could think straight or at least not make a fool out of myself when he was around. I was clean, waxed and ready for action with Ray.

We were finished with dinner at a restaurant in town and had just ordered a second cocktail, when my phone chimed with a text message. I looked down and read the message, my eyes widened with surprise. I looked up at Ray, then back down at my phone, then back up to Ray.

"Is something wrong?" he asked, looking concerned.

"Yes... I mean no, nothing's *wrong*... I just," I licked my lips and took a couple of gulps of my drink. "A friend came into town a day early, so I'll need to go on home." I could tell he was disappointed, but I was surprisingly not. "Raincheck though. Maybe... sometime this next week?"

"Okay, sure," he conceded, "Sounds good," he smiled sweetly. He really was a nice guy. I finished my drink *and* his as we made a plan for next time. My libido would just have to control itself.

Ray pulled up to my house as the sun was setting. Erik was sitting on the front porch swing with his arm slung across the back. He had on what he always wore, jeans, a white T-shirt, open flannel with a knit hat covering his dark hair. *Damn he looked good.*

"Is that your friend?" Ray asked, cocking his eyebrow at me.

"Yeah, Erik was actually Jake's best friend, so I kinda inherited him," I smiled and leaned over to give Ray a quick hug goodbye. He seemed surprised by my lack of affection, but I wasn't going to kiss him with Erik ogling us from his perch. "See you later this week."

"See you later," he said as I closed the door. I smiled at Erik as I walked up to the porch. He got up to meet me and wrapped his arms around me in a huge hug. I wondered for a split second what Ray would think since he was still backing down the drive, but those thoughts melted away with Erik's arms around me. *He smelled good.*

"I've missed you," I murmured against his chest. We pulled back and both took seats on the front porch swing. "What are you doing out here all by your lonesome?"

"Waiting on you, love," he smiled, "and smoking." He handed me the joint he had lit. "I've missed you too. Is that the local bloke that your mate talked about?" he asked, pointing a finger at the driveway.

"That's him," I replied. *Damn his good memory.* Erik looked delectable with his arm slung over the back of the swing, his body turned toward me. I would have loved to snuggle up against him as he slowly moved our swing back and forth with his foot. Taking a long drag from the joint, I settled on leaning back against the arm of the swing and swung my legs up next to him.

Erik placed his hand on my leg and squeezed. "I guess he's your *boyfriend* now," he taunted.

"What am I, sixteen?" I laughed and shook my head. "*No,* he's not my *boyfriend.* We've only gone out a few times." I took another long drag and handed the joint back to Erik.

"It's been three bloody months and you've only gone out a few times?" he laughed in surprise. "I've seen snails move faster." He pulled my rainboots off my feet and dropped them on the floor below. I raised an eyebrow wondering what he had planned, then closed my eyes and groaned with pleasure as he started massaging my socked feet. *Nearly as good as sex. Nearly.*

"Foot rubs are my favorite," I sighed with my eyes still closed. His hands seemed to pinpoint every little knot and melt it away, combining it with my high was heavenly.

"I know," he murmured. I opened my eyes and met his warm gaze with a half-smile. "Is he your friend with benefits then?" *He DOES have a good memory.*

"I had planned on sealing the deal tonight after our date, but *someone* decided to come a day early," I closed my eyes again to enjoy the massage, but Erik's hand had stopped moving. I opened my eyes and he was staring forward, lost in thought. "Hey…" I reassured, wiggling my feet, "I'm just kidding. I'm really glad you're here."

"You were going to fuck him, but you came home early for me?" I couldn't tell if he was happy about my decision or not. I grabbed the joint that he had yet to toke and fired another hit.

"*Fuck* is not the term I would use with him, but yeah basically." I chuckled and gave a little shrug, "I wanted to see you."

"I *needed* to see you," he smirked and began massaging my feet again. *Hallelujah!* "Why wouldn't you use the term fuck with this guy?" My eyes had started to close but popped back open with that question.

I thought for a few seconds before chuckling, "I don't know... He's just a *nice* guy." I took another greedy hit and handed him back the joint. "Maybe I'm wrong... maybe he's a lady in the streets and a freak in the sheets," I chuckled again. "Either way he'll get the job done." I guess the alcohol/weed/massage combo had loosened my tongue.

"Get the job done?" Erik howled and stomped his foot. "You mean orgasm? There's no way the bloke in that truck could give you a proper one." His laughter shook the whole swing.

"You know that just by looking at him through the windshield?" I asked skeptically, trying not to laugh.

"I'm an excellent judge of orgasms," he taunted as I rolled my eyes.

"Listen," I said, holding up a finger. "I feel like a horned-up teenager. One: I need to get laid. Two: A distraction, nothing exclusive. Three: No drama, just fun," I ticked each off on my fingers. "I think he can provide at least one of those," I concluded.

"You don't seem excited by him," Erik inferred. "I thought you said..." he paused for a second like he was trying to remember, "you needed to be fucked." My eyebrows shot up in shock, and he met my gaze with his best smirk. "Tell me I'm wrong," he taunted. *Fuck.* I snatched the joint from his hand and lit it, taking a long drag. *Two tears in a bucket... fuck it.*

"You're not wrong," I confessed as I exhaled. He took a deep breath.

"I believe *I* can provide all of those things that you need," he coaxed with that same sexy smirk. "A distraction, no drama... just fun."

"How?" I asked suspiciously, narrowing my eyes. Erik closed his eyes and dropped his head, shaking it back and forth.

"Jesus, Kelly… by *fucking* you," he growled. My eyes widened again. *Oh shit!* "Just think about it," Erik finally said. He moved my feet from his lap, got up, and went inside. I was still in shock swinging back and forth from the momentum of Erik's departure from the swing. *Did that really just happen?* I got up, grabbed my rain boots and followed him inside.

"You can't just throw shit like that out and walk off," I asserted. "Are you being serious?"

"I said to think about it. I can handle it if you can." He grabbed some leftovers out of the fridge. "Can I have these?" I nodded since words were foreign to me at the moment. My immediate thought was *Fuck yeah!* but it was coming from my groin and not my brain.

"I'll think about it," I conceded.

"It's sex not a dentist appointment… though, you will get drilled," he wiggled his eyebrows at me as he ate cold pasta salad straight from the container. The effects of the weed made me laugh a little too hard at his stupid joke. "Damn, this is good," he howled softly. I walked over and he held out his fork with a nice big bite of the cold salad. I looked up at him, unintentionally, as I accepted the bite he offered. It *was* good.

"Thanks," I smiled after I swallowed my bite. His eyes were smoldering as he looked down at my lips. I needed to wrap my brain around his offer, and he was far too tempting standing right in front of me. Distance, I needed distance. "Sit," I said, backing up and motioning to the bar stool on the other side of the kitchen island. "I said I'll think about it."

Erik sat down and took another bite of the pasta and swallowed before asking. "Are you still going to fu– have sex with that local bloke if you say yes to me?"

"Maybe," I hesitated, shocked that we were even discussing this so casually. "Do you want me to tell you if I do?"

He shrugged. "I don't think so. Would you want me to tell you if *I* do?"

"Have sex with that local bloke?" I teased as he rolled his eyes. He set the empty container down on the counter and looked at me directly, making his words very clear.

"Do you want me to tell you if I fuck anyone besides you?"

My breath hitched as I thought about it for a moment before replying. "*IF*, we do then I wouldn't think so," I glanced at the clock and was surprised at the time. "Crap! It's late. We better call it a night," I said somberly. I wasn't ready for the night to end, but I wasn't ready to make a possible life-altering decision either because of my libido.

"I guess we should. Too bad I'm not that knackered," he hinted.

"Me either," I smiled innocently. "You want to watch TV in my room?" Erik's eyebrows shot up. "*Just* watch TV," I reminded.

Erik laughed, "I'll take what I can get. Be back down in a jif." He ran upstairs. *Oh shit. I'm playing with fire.*

I was brushing my teeth when Erik came back downstairs. He leaned against the door jamb of the bathroom wearing his signature tight, white T-shirt and plaid pajama pants and watched me complete my nighttime routine.

"Still want to fuck me?" I asked with my mouth full of toothpaste and my hair piled on top of my head.

"More than ever, love," he laughed out loud. I rolled my eyes and finished up while he waited. "What do you want to watch?" he asked as we headed back to the bedroom. I would have loved the feeling of being so comfortable with someone, but the butterflies in my stomach disagreed with me.

"What would you guess since you know me *so* well?" I teased. We laid on top of the comforter and grabbed a throw blanket from the foot of the bed.

"You're high, so… *Vacation,*" he smirked. *Dammit.*

"You don't mind watching it again? We can watch something else if you want." I found the movie on Prime and started it, then gave him my sweetest smile. I had probably seen this movie a hundred times, so I wouldn't blame Erik for wanting to watch something else.

"I don't mind a bit," he murmured. "What if I fall asleep?" he asked dreamily.

"It's okay… I don't mind a bit," I said softly. Our hands touched underneath the blanket and our fingers intertwined. We were both asleep before the movie even started.

The alarm woke me the next morning to find my head on Erik's chest, his arms around me. I felt so well rested. I reached for the phone to turn my alarm off as Erik stretched and moaned out what sounded like a 'good morning'. His arm was still under my head, so I rolled back towards him, and he pulled me close.

"Good morning," I smiled, rubbing my eyes. "How did you sleep?"

"Very well, and you?" he murmured, rubbing his hand up and down my back.

"*Very* well," I chuckled. "I have breakfast to set out in the lobby. I'll be your best fri—end if you lend me a han—nd," I said in a sing-song type voice as I looked up at him. Erik didn't have to leave until noon, so he had some time.

"You *are* my best friend," he murmured, keeping his eyes closed. He must not have shaved for a while since the scruff on his face was longer than I had seen him wear it. He looked so sexy in my bed, even with his clothes on. Erik opened his eyes and smiled warmly, watching my face as he tucked some of my hair behind my ear. "But I'll help you anyway," he added.

I could feel my heart rate pick up as we looked at one another. "Thank you," I replied, thoughts of what his lips would feel like flooded my mind. We leaned towards one another. *Fuck! Is this about to happen?*

My phone in my hand started blaring out a horrible beeping sound, which meant that was my final warning to get up. We both jumped at the sound, with the mood broken. I went to the bathroom as Erik headed to the kitchen and started the coffee pot. I splashed water on my face to clear my head. *Why wouldn't I pull the trigger on this? I had no idea. Was I intimidated? Hell yes, he's way younger than I am with a body that won't stop. Was I scared? Yes! I loved our relationship and fucking him would be a gamble.* I threw my hair up in a messy bun and went to help Erik in the kitchen.

"How was your trip to England?" I asked Erik as I refilled his coffee mug. We had finished putting out the continental breakfast platters in the reception area for the cabin guests, and I had just refilled the coffee dispenser.

"Brilliant," he lit up and took a seat. "It was good to see my mum. Her last report came out well, and her cancer is still in remission. I've missed everyone... even my dim brothers," he grinned. "The two oldest have grandkids now, isn't that wild?"

"That *is* wild," I replied. I forgot that Erik's siblings were around my age.

"My mum and sister want to make a trip over, just the two of them," he hedged.

"That would be fun!" I exclaimed, clapping my hands. "I'd love to meet them. You would bring them out here, right?"

"I knew you'd be excited," he grinned, with a knowing wink. "This is the only place they want to come, since they've been to Seattle a few times before," he smiled, wistfully. "I might have mentioned you a time or two," he confessed, flashing me his sexy smirk.

"Pick a date and we'll make it happen. They can stay here in the big house with us. Ooo, I can't wait!" I was downright giddy. The idea of meeting the women that helped mold Erik into the man he was, was intriguing.

He laughed at my excitement. "Easy there, Miss Fancypants. Nothing is booked yet, so it will be a while... but I'm happy you're excited."

I returned his smile from the safety of the opposite side of the kitchen island. "So, you got some good quality time in with your mom?" I asked. He responded with a wide smile.

"I really did. She's always given me good advice about life, so I'm doing what *you* said and listening to *her*," he said cryptically and took a sip of his coffee.

"What did she say?" I asked sincerely. For whatever reason, I was desperate to know.

"To follow my gut and do what makes me happy," he smiled and took another sip.

"Good advice." *I like this woman.*

"I thought so," he smiled. Erik told me more about his trip home and details about his nieces and nephews and now a grandniece and grandnephew. He asked about my time away, so I updated him on my kids, family and friends. Erik and I had been having such a good conversation that neither of us had checked the time.

"Oh shit! I have to go," Erik swore as he grabbed his plate, ran over and placed it in the sink. He kissed me on the cheek. "I'll see you tomorrow night, love." He turned and raced upstairs.

"Have a good ride!" I yelled after him and began to finish cleaning the kitchen.

"I'll show *you* a good ride!" I heard him yell as the bedroom door slammed shut.

I hate allergies. I especially hate allergies that turn into sinus infections. I felt miserable by the time Saturday evening rolled around. The doctor wasn't available until Monday, so I had to self-medicate at home. Blankets were piled on top of me to get rid of my chill, and Larry (*bless his heart)* was handling my job *and* his. A light knock on my door caught my attention, but I was too tired to say anything.

"Hey. Are you alright, love?" I opened my eyes to see Erik squatting next to me by the bed. He still had his bicycle gear on, so he must have just gotten back.

"No," I croaked. He handed me a glass of water and helped me take a drink. The cool water felt good and helped my dry throat immediately. "Thanks."

"Do you need anything?" He was touching my face with the back of his hand. Concern was etched all over his sexy face.

I tried to smile. "I'm good," I uttered huskily. Erik helped me take another sip of water.

"I'll check on you again in a bit… after I see if Larry needs any help. Will you let me know if you need anything?" I only nodded as he cupped my cheek in his hand and stroked my face with his thumb. His firm touch felt so good since the sinus pressure was so strong. I closed my eyes and moaned.

"Does that feel good?" he asked in surprise. I could only nod again and point at either side of my nose. He started massaging where I had pointed, and it relieved some of the pressure I was feeling. I moaned again. I'd kiss him right then if I had the energy, but I couldn't even open my eyes. He was still massaging my face when I fell asleep.

Overcast skies were all I could see out my window when I opened my eyes. I had no idea what time it was. Hell, I didn't know what *day* it was! The clock on my bedside table read 10:15. *Shit!* Breakfast was late. I started to get out of bed, but my body reminded me of why I was there. I still ached all over. Wrapping my softest blanket around my shoulders, I walked out to peek into the lobby area. Breakfast was all set out for the guests just like I normally do it. *Wow!* I waddled into the living area, and there in the kitchen were Larry and Erik talking and laughing while they cleaned together. They were so absorbed in their conversation and work that they didn't notice when I sat quietly on the couch. I couldn't quite make out their conversation, due to the music Erik was playing on his phone, but I loved how engaged they were in each other. They must have set the breakfast service together, which made me smile.

"I think she's still out of it," Erik said to Larry as he walked towards me.

I cleared my mind and tried to focus on Erik's face. "I'm feeling better actually. Just a little achy still," I pulled the blanket closer around me as a chill made me shiver. "I took an edible and I'll go back to sleep after it kicks in. Did y'all put out breakfast for me?" I asked, trying to smile.

Larry's toothy grin told me I was right. "We didn't want you to have to worry about it," he consoled. Erik gave me a wink.

"Thanks, y'all. I really appreciate it." I started to get up, but Erik came over and took my elbow to steady me.

"I'll get her settled, mate. We'll talk later," Erik called to his partner in crime.

"I'll see myself out," Larry responded, then I heard the front door close.

"I'm not keeping you from anything, am I?" I asked as Erik helped me back into bed. It had been nice getting up and stretching my legs, but I was already exhausted.

"Nothing at all, love. I planned on staying until Monday already," he soothed. "But in much different circumstances," he mumbled as he adjusted my pillows.

"Yeah, not having to take care of sick, pathetic *me*," I grumbled.

"Oh, I planned on taking care of you," he murmured as he climbed next to me in bed and pulled me into his arms. I laid against his chest as he rubbed my face like he did before. I hummed beneath his strong fingers; it was heaven to my aching face.

I gave a little laugh as I thought about what he was implying, "You mean sex, right?"

"Yeah, I do," he murmured and kissed the top of my head.

"I'm still thinking about it," I mumbled, trying to keep my eyes open.

"You think too much," he grumbled.

The sun was setting when I woke up again. I was still wrapped in Erik's arms, and he was watching a funny movie that made him chuckle.

"Have you been lying here with me all day?" I asked sleepily, sitting up to assess how I felt.

"A lot of it, but not all day," he grinned. "You sound better."

"I feel better. I think I'll go take a shower," I looked down at Erik's lips and bit my own. "I bet that'll help." I stepped into the bathroom and started the shower. I thought for a moment, then left the bathroom door unlocked. *I won't say no if he comes in.* I took a long, leisurely shower without hearing a peep from outside the door.

Erik was waiting when I got out of the bathroom with homemade chicken soup from June and crackers. We sat in bed and watched TV and talked all night, until we fell asleep together again.

Elyse Rundell

Chapter 13

Present Day...

"You think y'all would have gone all the way if you hadn't gotten sick?" Sam gasped.

"I think we would have! Am I crazy?" I asked, already knowing what her answer would be.

"Hell no! I think you should do him and not look back," she exclaimed, throwing her hands in the air. Sam lowered her voice. "Listen, I know you... you'll regret it if you don't," she added. "It says a lot that you left a sure thing like Ray the Local to go home to him... even though you knew Erik wasn't going anywhere."

I took a deep breath. "Exactly what I was thinking," I sighed. "I didn't even have to make a choice. It was obvious that I needed to come home." I leaned back in my lounge chair and stared up at the darkening sky.

"Did you see Ray later that week?" Sam asked, taking a sip of her drink. "Did you get laid?" I took a few sips of my drink before answering as she eyed me suspiciously.

"Yep, well... kinda," I replied sheepishly.

"Kinda?" she asked exasperated.

"Let's just say," I took another sip of my drink, "it was nothing to write home about." Sam's eyes grew huge. She jumped up in her seat, and I thought for a second she was going to jump on me.

"What!?" she exclaimed in a loud whisper. "You had *sex* and you're just *now* telling me about it?" She took another sip of her cocktail. "It must have been awful," she hissed.

"Not *awful*," I smirked, "just very... uneventful. Jake and I had a fun, active sex life before he got sick," I sighed. "I'm needing some excitement!" I laughed while giving a shimmy to my shoulders. "Oh shit, here he comes!"

"The excitement?" Sam laughed.

"Hell yeah!" I exclaimed, laughing.

"I need more details about the uneventful sex," Sam whispered as the door started to open.

"Later," I hissed as I tried my best to look casual.

"Tell me why I do this again?" asked Erik as he came back out the door after delivering the Asshole's food.

"Because it pays for your expensive hobbies," I quoted him back to himself. He always seemed to be getting new gear for whatever new guide trip he was planning... attachments for the kayaks, new shocks for his mountain bike, lighter camping equipment for hiking. *I get tired just thinking about it.*

"That's right," he grinned. "The Arseholes and I will head out early in the morning. Can someone pick us up in Forks at four?"

I gave him a mock salute. "Aye, aye captain!" Erik raised his middle finger in my direction as he took another bite of his food. Laughing, I went inside to clean up the kitchen after the dinner spread. Through the open door, I could hear Erik and Sam talking...

"Are you hitting the trail with us tomorrow? We always have room for an extra," Erik asked.

"Ha! Thanks, but no thanks. Looking at a man's ass in front of me all day is not my idea of a good time," Sam replied, making Erik laugh. "But seriously, Kelly said you've been a good friend to her since Jake passed... thanks for that."

"I like to think I was a good friend even before Jake passed but thank you. She means a lot to me." I stopped what I was doing and listened intently.

"You mean a lot to her too," said Sam. I took a step closer to the door.

"She told you that?" Erik asked, lowering his voice.

"In so many words," Sam replied. I took another step towards the door glad I hadn't turned on any music.

"I wish... I hoped..." Erik stammered. *Damn my bad hearing!* I took another step closer, craning my neck as far as I could. "Kelly would..."

"FUCK!!!" I yelled as I slid sideways falling flat on my side. *Damn these stupid socks!* Erik and Sam ran inside just as I rolled to my back cringing in pain and a little humiliation.

"Are you hurt? What happened?" Erik asked wide-eyed with concern.

"I slid on these damn floors in these stupid socks," I muttered. Erik offered his hand to help me up. I was nearly up when my still-socked feet went flying, landing me flat on my ass this time. "FUCK!" I yelled again. I looked up for Erik's help but both he and Sam were on the floor. *What the hell?* I tore off the wretched socks and clamored to my feet. They were... *laughing!?* My mouth fell open. Erik was on his knees, doubled over, hitting the ground, tears rolling down his face. Sam was sitting on her side, apparently having fallen down from the laughter and finding it hard to breathe since she too was crying. "Fuck y'all," I gasped. I flipped them both off and walked over to finish cleaning up the kitchen.

"I'm so sorry, love. I'm so sorry," Erik choked out, still trying to catch his breath from his laughing attack. He came over to me at the sink and placed his hand on my cheek. "How are you?" he asked, trying to sound sincere.

I held his stare for a second before answering, "I'm fine. Just slightly humiliated." I jerked my head away.

Erik shook his head and laughed, "Your humility could stand a hit."

"Good point," I chuckled and rubbed my sore hip. I'd probably feel that more tomorrow. Having finally composed herself from her laughing fit enough to chat, Sam entertained us with stories of her lesbian conquests while I finished cleaning the kitchen.

"Done! I'm going to watch the stars. Who's in?" I asked as I tucked the dish towel away and grabbed my half-full cocktail. I walked back out onto the deck and resumed my place on my favorite lounger. Lying back gave the perfect view of the night sky and all its glory.

"This is nice," cooed Sam as she eased onto the matching chair. "I've missed this."

"It *is* lovely," sighed Erik as he sat down again on the end of my chair, "too bad I bodge my neck when I try to look up." He looked over at me shrewdly and rubbed his neck. I raised a questioning eyebrow in response.

"Do you want to lay down?" I asked hesitantly.

"Don't mind if I do," he practically sang as he twisted around onto his back and snuggled his hips between my legs, cushioning his head between my boobs. "Thank you." I wasn't sure what to do, how to move, or what to say. My gaze drifted to Sam who's baffled expression matched my own. Laying back, I tried to steady my breathing. *Relax, Kelly. He's just a man. A sexy, sexy man but still just a man.* That helped. It really was a comfortable position. Falling asleep would have been easy if all of my nerve endings weren't on fire. Every point of contact that my body made with his was crackling. I was sure he could feel my heart beating out of my chest beneath his head.

"I've got to see a man about a horse… plus I'm pooped. I'm calling it a night. Good night y'all," chirped Sam as she jumped up and skipped inside, throwing a wink over her shoulder at me as she passed through the open door.

Erik looked up at me puzzled. "That's Sam," I laughed nervously. Even upside down he was gorgeous. It would be so easy for him to flip around and kiss me, then ravage me right here on my favorite chair. *Stop, Kelly. Get it together.* Though, it hadn't escaped my attention that Erik stayed between my legs instead of grabbing the now vacant chair to my side. I let out a long, cleansing breath. "What's new with you?"

"Not a lot. Work has taken up a lot of my time lately." He updated me on his latest project, and we chatted about our last two weeks apart as time ticked away, without Erik making a move. *Was he going to say anything or was he waiting on me?* Glancing at the time, it seemed too late for us to start anything tonight. I took another deep breath.

"How are you? Am I hurting you?" Erik asked in a whisper-soft voice.

"There's that question again. I'm fine," I said a little too gruffly. "Though I am enjoying this little cuddle sesh, you have an early day tomorrow." *So that came out a little too snarky.*

"True… Anyway we could do this again tomorrow tonight? I might have just found my new favorite seat." Erik slowly got up and stretched his tall, lean body from side to side. His shirt rode up to show the ridge that followed his hips down past the waistband of his jeans. *I wonder what he would taste like if I followed it down with my tongue.*

"I– I'm sure we can make that happen," I stammered. "You know where to find me."

"I do. It's a date," he smiled and leaned down, kissing the top of my head, "Good night."

"Good. Night." I said slowly but he was already gone.

"What in the actual hell, Kelly!?" shrieked Sam when I gave her the play-by-play the next morning. Erik and his Assholes left straight from our farm for the trail, so they'd been gone for a while already. Sam had just gotten up and was preparing her coffee when I came in from my morning chores. I was holding my breath waiting for her reaction. "You have a cuddle date planned for tonight?" she asked before busting out in laughter. "Quit being such a chicken! Something could have totally happened last night if you hadn't freaked out."

"Right?" I moaned, then matched her laughter with my own. "I don't need a fucking 'cuddle' date." I blanched just at the thought of having him between my thighs again without any relief. "It's my own damn fault. Is there a female equivalent for blue balls?"

"I think it's just soaked panties," Sam laughed. "Tell him you accept his offer and give yourself some satisfaction!"

"What do I say? Yo! Erik! I accept your offer. Let's get– it– on," I laughed as I thrust my hips with each word.

"I swear, you're still fourteen," Sam groaned as she rolled her eyes. "Just go with whatever flow he is throwing at you. Now give me the deets on the boring sex with Ray the Local."

I looked at the clock and still had plenty of time before I had to leave with the transport van. "Fine, it happened last week when we met up for our raincheck. Ray made me dinner at his place."

Chapter 14

One Week Ago...

Ray's lavender farm was breathtaking. Its fields of various shades of purple stretched across the prairie with the Olympic Mountains towering behind, their peaks still capped with snow, made the perfect backdrop for any occasion. This part of the Olympic Peninsula is known for its lavender farms, and Ray's was one of the prettiest. I had just parked in his driveway and was following the path to the backyard when I stopped to admire the scenery.

"I never get tired of this view," said Ray as he walked up next to me and placed his hand on the small of my back.

"I don't either," I sighed and turned, meeting his smile. "What's for dinner? I'm starving!"

He turned and cocked his arm for me to slide my arm through. "Right this way," he smiled and led me down a path through the lavender field. I saw a lone table was candlelit, underneath a metal-framed arbor where purple gauze curtains were bellowing in the breeze. It was the most romantic location I had ever seen.

"I hope you are charging people good money for this!" I gawked. "Romantic settings like this would have a waitlist for months." I looked around at the sweeping view and envisioned white-clothed tables spread throughout the lavender field like an open-air, high-end restaurant.

"It is one of the ideas I have been tossing around," he volunteered as he pulled a chair out for me to sit down. "Chardonnay?" he asked as he poured the chilled wine into the goblets on the table.

"You know I do," I retorted, leaning back in my chair. I took a sip of the cool, crisp wine as I raised an eyebrow and looked at Ray. "Pulling out all the stops. You do remember that I'm not wanting anything serious, right?"

"I remember," he smiled and took a seat to the right of me at the table. "Can't a guy practice doing something romantic?"

I raised my brow even more skeptically. "As long as it's only practice," I sighed and looked around, "Because this is fabulous, and I want you to use it for someone who'll appreciate it."

"Kelly, you've made your intentions clear," Ray said, waving me off as he got up from the table. "Please let me feed you. I'll be right back with our food." He turned and walked toward his house presumably to get our plates. I downed the rest of my glass of wine and grabbed the bottle to fill it again, glad to see that another bottle was chilling close by. Ray came back quickly with our plates, and we enjoyed our dinner chatting amicably about how he could market this experience.

"You're over your two-drink max," I laughed as Ray emptied the wine bottle and was opening the third that he brought back from his house.

"True," he huffed as he pulled up the cork from the bottle, "But I don't have to drive anywhere." He had a good point. The ball was in my court, and I had to choose. I could either keep drinking and stay the night or switch to water and leave sooner rather than later. No way was I going to do this sober. *Fuck it.* I pushed my empty glass towards Ray.

"I don't *have* to drive anywhere either," I winked, and he smiled warmly at me as he took my hand. We decided to take the bottle with us and forego the glasses, as Ray gave me an impromptu tour of his lavender barn. I doubt an inch was missed as he went into detail about every step in the harvest process. I wasn't sure if he was nervous or just *that* into his work. It did smell heavenly with the bouquets of lavender hanging upside down drying in columns. Finally, Ray drew me close and nuzzled my neck as he ended the tour. The wine must be loosening his inhibitions.

"You smell as good as the lavender," he murmured in my ear. *Really? I doubt that, but who am I to argue?*

"Thanks," I murmured back as he kissed my lips softly. I leaned forward to increase the pressure and nudged my tongue against his lips, but Ray shifted back with a chuckle.

"Whoa, slow down," he chuckled again. "Let's walk back to the house where we can get more comfortable."

I grinned and leaned forward again. "We can always start here," I whispered in his ear as I kissed down his neck. *Let's get this party started.* Ray laughed nervously and ducked away from me, grabbing the big door of the barn and pulling it open.

"Oh, I'd feel better if we went inside," he smiled, though he looked like he might jump if I said "boo".

"It's okay, Ray, breathe," I soothed. "We don't have to do anything you're not comfortable with." I suddenly felt like the creepy guy from a frat party that's trying to get into the sorority girl's pants.

"I'm okay, really. I'm just more of a bedroom kind of guy," he smiled shyly.

"Okay, sure. Is anyone home?" I asked as we walked out of the barn and back towards Ray's house. I hugged his arm as we walked to warm myself against the cool air.

"The kids are with their mom," he said. Ray had been divorced for a couple of years, and his ex-wife lived just down the road from his farm. He tipped the bottle up, finishing our third bottle of wine. Regrettably, he had consumed considerably more of that last bottle than I had. We walked inside his house chatting about his kids as I glanced around his home. It had potential but definitely needed some interior design help… and furniture, only having a couch and coffee table in the center of the room. Ray grabbed the television remote, turning on the massive set that took up nearly an entire wall. "Have a seat. I'll just turn something on while we open another bottle." *He could get to turning ME on.*

"You know what sounds like more fun?" I asked mischievously with a twinkle in my eye. I walked closer and took the remote from his hand.

"What?" he asked, returning my smile with a bit of confusion.

"Making out."

Ray coughed at my blunt response and chuckled before walking to the kitchen, grabbing a couple of water bottles from a stack of cases he had by his fridge. "You *are* direct," he said as he handed me one of the bottles.

"I'm more of a grab the bull by the horns kinda gal," I smirked as Ray leaned forward and softly kissed my lips. I dropped the bottle on a table, grabbed the front of Ray's shirt with both hands and pulled him toward me, deepening our kiss. I needed some action, and my patience was beginning to wear thin. Ray backed up, grabbing my hands.

"Let's go in here," he breathed, motioning toward the hallway. I followed him to his bedroom, where I was happy to see that at least he had bedroom furniture. *Fuck yeah, here we go.* I stood by the bed while Ray turned off the lights, the outside lights shown through the window allowing our silhouettes to be seen. Ray fumbled with the fastener on my jeans as we kissed in the dark. I helped him unbutton the unwanted barrier and pushed them down to the ground along with my panties. He pushed his own pants down as I laid down on the bed then he climbed on top of me and kissed my lips softly. "Ready?" he asked quietly as he kissed my mouth again.

"I think so…" I said. *Did he mean for sex? Already?* I felt his erection pressing between my legs as Ray shifted his hips. *No foreplay?* "Uh, could we make out for a little longer or something? I need a little more… stimulation," I persuaded as I wiggled against him.

"Sure, sure," he murmured as he kissed me again, a little firmer than before. I plunged my tongue into his mouth causing him to moan, but I wasn't entirely sure if it was with pleasure or not. I moved my body against his, pushing my middle against his hardness to increase the friction. "Now?" he gasped as the tip of his shaft brushed against my opening.

"Sure," I said, hoping that his moves would make up for the lack of foreplay. They didn't. He fumbled with a condom, entered me swiftly, thrust four times before making a guttural growl and finishing before we barely began. I didn't even have time to *fake* an orgasm. Ray let out a long, deep breath as he lay there looking at the ceiling. *I guess he's done.* Erik's words from the week before came back to haunt me. Maybe he *was* a good judge of who could give an orgasm. I slowly rolled off the bed and got to my feet as Ray sat up.

"Where are you going?" he asked as I slid my panties and pants back up my legs. "Weren't you going to spend the night?"

"I'm good. It's not too late and I'm sober, so I'll just head home." *Do I tell him he's lousy in bed?*

"That was fun. We should do it again some time," I looked up to see if he was being sarcastic, but the expression on his face showed sincerity.

"Remember, Ray. I'm just wanting a friend... nothing more." *Especially from you.* He was such a nice guy, but he was not a good match for me. Ray put on his pants and walked me to my jeep with a quick kiss goodbye. I made the slow trek home being mindful of the wildlife that made a habit of jumping onto the road. After nearly thirty years of being with the same man, I had *finally* had sex with someone else... and it was *so* disappointing. After getting zero relief for my libido, Erik's offer looked even more intriguing.

Elyse Rundell

Chapter 15

Present Day...

I was waiting at the Forks trailhead that afternoon to pick up Erik and his Assholes. I had front row parking; the windows were down, and the music was up. I was enjoying this exceptionally sunny day on this part of the Peninsula. I checked my reflection one last time, feeling like a damn teenager. At least Sam had been nice for the rest of the morning and not given me too hard of a time about Boring Sex Ray or last night with Erik.

Not long after four, Erik's group pulled in. I'd recognize those legs… I mean, his bicycle anywhere. I watched as he stopped pedaling and sat straddling his bicycle talking to a couple of the other guys in the group. He reached down, grabbed the hem of his shirt and pulled it over his head. I could feel the moisture building in my panties as my eyes traveled up his rippled torso. My nipples hardened as I wondered what his skin tasted like hot and sweaty. He wiped his neck with his shirt, and I wished I was that shirt as I bit my lip and watched it glide across his smooth skin. I glanced up right into his god-damned smirking eyes. "Fuck," I muttered, glad I wasn't a man since I would be sporting a huge boner right now.

Erik dismounted and walked his bike over, never breaking eye contact. "Enjoying the view or is the jury still out?"

"Deja vu, huh?" I smiled as my heart pounded out of my chest. "And I'm not complaining about the view."

"You better not, love. I work hard keeping this *girlish* figure," he purred as he squeezed one of his nipples.

"Worth every minute," I laughed. "Now get your sexy ass in this van."

"Yes, ma'am," he pretended to tip a hat then yelled, "You heard the boss, load up!" Erik came back around after he loaded his bicycle and leaned into my open window. "Do you mind if we take a couple of extra cyclists back with us and drop them in Sequim?"

"No problem. It'll be tight but we have the room." I started taking items off the middle console, so we could have an additional seat. I looked up just as Erik was scooting across the bench seat in my direction. "Did you draw the short straw?" I laughed as he scooted closer. My mouth suddenly felt like it was full of cotton.

"You think I'd let one of these knobs sit so close to you?" he muttered under his breath. We started the uncomfortable trip back home with Erik pressed up against me. I noticed there was plenty of room between him and the Asshole on his right, but I decided not to mention it.

"Did you have to leave your shirt off?" I feigned disgust but my wet panties told a different story, as I took a glance sideways at his incredible body.

"You know you love it." He leaned closer and lowered his voice. "The two guys are giving you each twenty bucks for the ride." He leaned in even closer and whispered, "I'll have to take a shower before our 'date' later," he used air quotes for the term as I rolled my eyes.

"Oh yeah. I nearly forgot," I lied unconvincingly.

"I'd be happy to remind you later, love. Trust me," he murmured close to my ear.

Holy Fuck. It was like fucking Niagara Falls in my pants. Erik wasn't the only one that was going to need a shower... a cold one. One of the Assholes in the backseat asked about one of the rivers we passed, and I was happy for the distraction. I dove into tour guide mode giving everyone a dramatic story about local history... pausing only when a sharp turn pressed Erik's bare-chested body closer to mine or when he brushed something off his leg and the back of his hand glided along my bare leg. *Fucking Niagara Falls.*

We dropped the two tag-alongs off in Sequim and headed to the farm with forty dollars more in my pocket.

Erik had kept his seat next to me for the remainder of the drive, but I was not complaining, except when he put his shirt back on. We dropped the bikes off at the cabins (since there would be no scheduled ride in the morning) with instructions for the Assholes to be up at the main house at seven sharp for dinner. Larry was prepping a crab boil for the whole farm and that son of a bitch knew his way around a crab pot. "I'm going to go change, then see what help Larry needs," I said to Erik as we were walking into the house. Sam wasn't downstairs, so she must be with Larry.

"Why do you need to change?" asked Erik, giving me a quick look from head-to-toe. "You look good to me," he murmured. I really did need to change my panties then. What did Sam say? *Go with his flow.*

"Just need to freshen up. Don't you have a shower to take, stinky?" I wrinkled my nose to look convincing, but I was loving the masculine way his sweaty skin smelled.

"I do," he said, turning toward the stairs. "If only I had someone to wash my back!" he called as he ran up taking them two at a time.

"There should be a loofah!" I yelled after him… *but what I wouldn't give to be that loofah.* I went to my bedroom for new panties.

The crab boil was a delicious success. Larry's title as reigning Crab King was still securely in place. Nearly every guest on the farm was in attendance, and the brewery's fabulous ale and cider were flowing as well as the conversation. The string lights dangling from above gave an inviting glow to the space, and our patio heaters were just enough to keep the cool night air at bay. Sam was enjoying herself as well as the company of the sales rep from the brewery who had just thrown her long, blonde hair back over her shoulder, laughing at something Sam had said. *I'm sure Sam is eating that shit up.* She was the same gorgeous sales rep I had in mind when I went and asked this brewery to come out tonight. I smiled as I congratulated myself on my successful planning and pimpin' skills.

"I'd love to know what that wicked smile was for...," murmured a delicious, English accent right behind me, so close his breath tickled my ear. *So much for dry panties.*

"Honestly?" I asked, turning in my chair with an air of bravery.

"Of course," he responded, looking slightly concerned, taking a large pull from his beer.

"I was congratulating myself on my pimpin' skills." This must not have been the answer Erik was expecting. He spit his beer clear across the table laughing and coughing all at once. Luckily, no one was in his path. His reaction had me snorting with laughter. "You wanted the truth," I warned.

"That I did, love, that I did," he smiled sweetly, drawing my eyes to the twinkle in his eye. "And why do you deserve these accolades for your pimping?"

I laughed at his attempt at sincerity. "I asked this brewery for a deal because I knew the sales rep would be right up Sam's alley." I nodded my head in the direction of

Sam and the rep deep in conversation then broke into the "Matchmaker" song from *Fiddler on the Roof.*

"Matchmaker, matchmaker, make me a match, find me a find, catch me a catch..."

"Please, God, no," Erik moaned as I ran out of the words I knew and started improvising. "Please, make it stop," as he plugged his ears with his fingers.

"You're just jealous of my skills," I swooned, snapping my fingers in his face with each word. "Singin', pimpin', matchmakin'... the list goes on."

"Such a renaissance woman... what other skills have you not shown me?" he teased as he grabbed his beer and took another long drink, not taking his eyes away from mine.

Dammit. I could slide off this fucking chair. "I'm full of surprises," I said huskily, not meaning to exactly, but my mouth was suddenly so dry... probably due to the overabundance of moisture in my underwear. "I need another drink." I got up and went to the coolers for another beer. "Can I get anyone anything while I'm up?" I asked loudly to everyone. I also needed to get some distance between my vagina and Erik's devilish tongue. *What he could probably do with that tongue.* It seemed the entire table needed another round, so I was happy for the break.

The party was coming to a close and our crowd was disbursing in pairs. I hadn't seen where Sam and the beer rep went, but I had a sneaky suspicion we'd need another seat for breakfast in the morning. "Are you going in?" Erik asked in my ear once everyone had left. He was so close I could feel the warmth from his body.

"I'm ready when you are," I replied. I was still unsure about his intentions. Sure, we had upped our flirting game into unknown territory, but I wasn't so sure it was still a game. I glanced around to make sure we were alone and took a deep breath. *Go with his flow.*

"Starting now," he murmured, taking my hand, sliding his fingers between mine, Erik's thumb rubbed an unknown pattern on my skin. He pulled my hand to his lips and gently kissed where his thumb had been, while he stared into my eyes. *Holy shit. I'm going to explode.*

"Handholding, huh? Is this *that* kind of date?" I asked softly.

"I'm only showing you what friends with benefits could be like with me," he breathed as he kissed my hand again.

"Are we going back to the deck?" I asked hesitantly, barely able to breathe. We stood that way for a few seconds before Erik took a deep breath and smiled.

"That's the plan," he nearly growled, turning and grabbing a couple of more beers from the cooler. We began walking hand-in-hand toward the house. "I guess you were right about your matchmaking skills. I haven't seen Sam or her new friend for a while."

I fanned my face with my hand and faked a humble disposition, "I just saw an opportunity for two people with similar interests to meet and realize they are made for one another. I don't know… some *may* call me a hero," I said, flaring my arm dramatically.

"Yet others call you a pimp," Erik crowed, which got a belly laugh from me. He paused our walk while I caught my breath. "You are…" he said, catching my eyes with his, "the coolest person I know."

"I mean… I am pretty great," I smiled slyly.

"And humble too," he grinned with a wink.

"*Very* humble… for sure," I giggled. "You're not so bad yourself," I whispered, squeezing his hand then continued our walk to the house, feeling my heartbeat increase the closer we walked.

"Am I higher on that list than *Ray*?" He drug out the last word in a mocking tone.

"Nice," I muttered, rolling my eyes. "Who said anything about Ray?" I had been undecided on whether I was going to tell Erik that I had sex with Ray the Local, but apparently the decision was made for me.

"Rosalie," he smiled. "She seemed happy for you… though I would have thought you'd have told me yourself." Erik was looking down following the path as it led us back home. *Damn Larry and his pillow talk!*

"I thought you didn't want to know," I reminded him.

"I changed my mind," he murmured.

Rolling my eyes, I took a deep breath. *Fuck it.* "There's not much to tell…" I began. Erik stopped walking and looked at me expectantly, but I pulled his hand that was still holding mine. "Let's keep walking. We'll never get home at this rate." Erik resumed his pace while I continued, "So, like I said, not much to tell… We went out a few times, remember? You saw him a couple of weeks ago. We had great conversation, but the sex… It was boring… I have a feeling he wants there to be something more… I don't… so I'm not going to see him again. The end," I rambled and shrugged. "Now you're all caught up."

We made it back to the deck. Erik gallantly drew back his arm for me to have a seat in my lounge chair… *our* lounge chair. I sat down as he handed me one of the stolen beers from the cooler already open. He then opened one for himself as he sat down between my legs and laid back, his head resting on my chest… exactly like the night before. He hadn't said a word, and my stomach was starting to twist in knots.

Finally, Erik's sinful voice broke the silence, "What do you mean 'boring'?"

I took a breath, not realizing I was holding mine. I began combing my fingers through his hair like I had seen him do countless times. It was so silky soft as it fell through my fingers. *He could be in shampoo commercials. Enough stalling, Kelly!* "Uh, I don't know… Boring, as in no foreplay… strictly missionary… that sort of thing." Luckily, I'd never shied away from being open about my sex life. I was more interested in where he would take this line of questioning. I gave myself a silent pat-on-the-back for maintaining my grooming regime "down there" just in case. Erik's next question jolted me back to the present.

"Did you come?" he asked innocently, though there was nothing innocent happening in the furnace that was my vagina. I continued my finger play with his hair since his question made me stop everything. *Might as well jump on board the honesty train, Kelly.*

"Nope, not even close. And… let's just say… there wasn't a lot of *time* for me to either," I chuckled uncomfortably. "Besides, at my age, I don't want to have to teach someone how to pleasure me. I want to sit back and enjoy the ride."

Erik took a long pull from his beer and stared up at the night sky with a sigh. "I'm not usually one to say, 'I told you so,' but…" he chuckled.

"Shut up," I groaned as I playfully yanked his hair.

"Let me know when you have your ticket," he taunted.

My fingers stopped their massage and pulled free from his thick locks. "What ticket?" I asked, chuckling lightly, not understanding his joke.

Erik sat up and turned towards me with the full strength of his sexiest grin, his dark hair hung over one eye. "Ticket for *my* ride." *Choo, choo, mother fucker.*

We stared at each other for a moment, both trying to decide how to judge the others' reaction. "Quit messin' with me," I finally said. Rolling my eyes, I stood up, pushing away from Erik and went inside with my temptation hot on my heels.

"Why not give me a go? Sounds like Boring Ray has set the bar pretty low," he chuckled as he watched me tidy up the kitchen.

"I wasn't sure if you were serious. Do you need to check MILF off your sex fantasy 'to-do' list?" I laughed and shook my head. "I'm still thinking about it… but now… I'm going to bed."

Erik closed the gap between us in two steps. He held my cheek with one hand while he pulled me into his embrace with the other and whispered in my ear, "*Do* keep me in mind when you're lying in bed with your eyes closed thinking… of what I could do to you." *Fuck.* He let me go and backed up a couple of steps with that damn smirk still on his face.

"Do you care at all about our age difference?" I asked, shaking my head.

"I don't care how fucking old you are, silly woman," he huffed. "You are in need of something that I am willing and able to provide. We'll talk about it later… Good night, Kelly," he said as he started to head upstairs.

"Good night, Erik," I said, stopping at the bottom of the stairs still absorbing our last exchange. I wasn't sure what else to say.

He turned around and looked down. "Just so you know, I do not have any motherly thoughts about you whatsoever… just to be clear," he admitted.

"What *are* your thoughts about me?" *Let's just follow this honesty train off the cliff.*

He gave me his panty-dropping smirk from where he stood on the landing. "I'll *show* you next weekend," and he turned to continue up the stairs.

Huh? "Wait!" I hissed. "What's next weekend?"

Erik stopped and came back down a few steps, his eyes as wide as they possibly could be. "Are you serious? Please tell me you're joking."

"Sure! Next weekend is…" I wracked my brain. *Next weekend?* Erik's face was starting to turn a light shade of purple. *C'mon Kelly, think! Oh yeah!* "Duh! The fundraiser gala! Yeah, next weekend. I'm ready," I prattled.

Erik came down a couple more steps. "Seriously, are you ready? It's a big night for both of us." I could see that he was being serious. Erik was hoping to gain some different groups of clients for his guide service, and this gala would open a lot more doors for my bed and breakfast as well.

"Seriously, I'm ready." I turned my brain to work mode and gave my libido a rest. "I pick my fancy dress up from the cleaners at the beginning of the week. My hair appointment is at three at a salon down the street from your place on Saturday. I'm getting my makeup done there too. Then I'll head over to your place to get dressed, and we'll be at the gala by seven *sharp*." I took a breath and smiled, "I promise, I won't let you down."

A relieved smile crossed Erik's sexy face as he pushed his hair out of his face. "I have a feeling it will be a night to remember... Good night, love."

I took a moment to take him all in, "Good night," and turned around and went to my room as he continued upstairs. A little while later I was in bed, staring at the ceiling, knowing Erik was in the room right above mine. I closed my eyes, like he said, and thought of how his hair felt when I was touching it. How it would feel to wrap my fingers in it as he was doing delicious dances with his tongue on my center. Could he hear my vibrator through the thin ceiling? Part of me hoped he could as I came over and over again thinking of that gorgeous smirk above me.

Chapter 16

"We'll need another seat for breakfast," Sam grumbled as she stomped into the kitchen still wearing her pajamas.

"Already done. I saw Miss Beer Rep's car was still here when I got up," I winked, handing Sam a hot mug of coffee.

She wrapped her hands around the oversized mug and breathed in the caffeinated aroma, "I always forget how fucking cheery you are in the mornings. Miss Beer Rep's name is *Skyler*, thank you very much."

"Y'all seemed to have hit it off," I grinned as she took a seat at the kitchen island.

"We did... *many* times. And, since there are no rainbows shooting out of your vagina, I'm assuming I'm the only one that got laid last night," she said gruffly. Sam was not a morning person even after a night of amazing sex.

"No pipe was laid but some obstacles might have been cleared from the path, but I'll tell you more later," I had lowered my voice to a whisper as I heard heavy footsteps coming down the stairs. Louder I said, "You're welcome for the fix up. Should we go ahead and pack you up now to move up here?"

"Who's moving up here?" Erik asked, dropping his duffle bag on the floor as he reached for the cup of coffee in my outstretched hand. He breathed in the aroma similar to Sam and took a sip. "Thank you…" he murmured, holding my gaze a moment longer than appropriate.

"You're welcome," I murmured back before clearing my throat and cutting my eyes over to Sam. She was definitely awake now, watching our interaction over the mug she held to her mouth. "Sam's moving here after her incredible night of lovemaking with *Skyler*," I said in answer to Erik's question.

"Skyler must be the beer rep?" Erik asked.

"Was there another gorgeous lesbian at the crab boil that I missed?" Sam's voice dripped with sarcasm.

"Sorry, she's not a morning person," I said to Erik while throwing a look of disapproval at Sam. "You leaving?" I asked, giving a nod toward his duffle bag.

"Yeah, a couple of the Arseholes rode with me, so they have to get back today," he glanced at the clock. "So… I'll see you Saturday then?"

"Yep. I'll meet you at your place after my hair and makeup appointments, so around five I'd guess. I'll just need to change, and we'll go." I nearly forgot Sam was in the room until she cleared her throat.

"And where, pray tell, is it that y'all are going together dressed so *fancy?*" She sounded much less grumpy than she did just minutes before.

"A charity gala in Seattle. I've got this gorgeous midnight blue gown. I'll tell you about it later," I reassured, giving Sam a wave of my hand.

"A charity gala that I had to remind her about last night," laughed Erik.

I shot him a glowering look, "It was only a temporary lapse of forgetfulness. I didn't think about it being so close. I swear I'm ready!"

"I'm ready too," Erik murmured, sending a smoldering look in my direction. It was hard not to miss the double entendre. Wetness pooled in my panties as I took a quick sip of my piping hot coffee. I'd get dehydrated if I stayed around this delicious man much longer. The sound of footsteps came from above, and Skyler bounded down the steps. "I do need to go," groaned Erik. "Skyler," he nodded at our latest arrival. "I'm Erik, nice to meet you... Sam, nice to meet you as well. I'm sure I'll see you again soon."

"I'll walk you out," I said, patting Erik's back. Skyler and Sam barely acknowledged Erik's greeting, only having eyes for each other. I spoke quietly as I walked him to the door after he slung his bag over his shoulder. "I was joking earlier about Sam moving up here, but it might not be so far-fetched seeing them now. I'll try not to get my hopes up." I smiled as we stopped on the front porch, and he turned to face me.

"Crazier things have happened... I hope you have a great week," Erik said, holding my gaze with his warm stare.

"*You* have a great week," I said, still holding his stare with my own.

Erik glanced around, dropped his bag, then slowly raised his hands and placed them on either side of my neck. He leaned down, bringing my face closer as his thumbs rubbed my cheeks. *What the–?* His gaze fell to my lips as his tongue licked his own in anticipation. Our lips touched for the briefest of moments before he smiled and backed away, letting his arms fall to his side. "I'll see you Saturday," he sighed, grabbed his bag and got in his SUV. *Fucking Niagara Falls.* I couldn't speak. I could only stare as he started his truck and our eyes met through the windshield. I'm not sure how long I stood there... leaning against the porch post, eyes locked with a man that made my womanly parts sing, and he'd hardly even laid a finger on me.

He held my stare, but I wasn't going to be the one to look away. We were playing a sexy game of chicken, and I was all in. Without breaking eye contact, Erik opened his door. I pushed myself off the porch post and took a small step forward. He got out of his truck; I took another step forward. It only took us three quick steps for our mouths to collide with one another. Our tongues danced magically together, giving and taking, like we had kissed a hundred times before but still needed more. I couldn't breathe and he was my oxygen. Our hands were sliding over each other's bodies, not stopping even for a moment. Erik finally tore his mouth away and took a step back. I took a step back as well, breathing heavily. We needed space between us or else we'd explode on the spot. "I'll see you Saturday," he said again, grinning as he turned back around and got in his truck.

"Looking forward to it!" I yelled nearly breathless as he backed out and headed down the driveway. *I need fresh panties.*

"Spill it!" Sam shrieked as soon as I came back into the kitchen. I spent the rest of the morning, after Erik left, giving both she and Skyler a rundown of what had happened the night before, just now on the porch, and even threw in more of Ray the Local for good measure, while I plied them with fresh fruit and homemade quiche hot from the oven. "SO hot!" Sam groaned.

"The quiche or the story?" laughed Skyler.

"Both! But I was talking about the sexual energy between y'all two. Wowza!" Sam fanned herself with her napkin.

"Smart to bring up the boring sex too," chimed Skyler.

"That wasn't part of my plan, but it could have nice consequences," I joked.

Sam threw her napkin at me from across the breakfast bar. "I still can't believe you didn't tell me about Boring Sex Ray!"

Laughing, I caught her napkin and threw it back. "Nothing to tell. And I mean *nothing*. He was really nice but... lacked creativity. No foreplay, no fun... no thank you."

"Why didn't anything happen last night with Erik? It sounds like you chickened out again." Sam asked the question I had already asked myself.

"I did... I'll admit it," I confessed. "I think I was waiting for him to make a move, but he was probably waiting for me to give him my decision. I know it's not a business transaction, but I want to set some parameters... Basically, I want him to fuck the shit out of me... Without it being weird and without everyone finding out about it. Is that too much to ask?" I pleaded mockingly.

"And you're fine with *him* seeing other people?" asked Skyler skeptically.

"As long as he doesn't bring anyone here, and I don't have to hear about it. Out of sight, out of mind... I guess," I shrugged, contemplating different scenarios in my head. "Oh! And I would want him to promise to use protection with anyone else. I don't want to have to mess with any of that shit."

"Would *you* date other people?" Sam inquired this time.

"Date? Sure." I pondered. "Though, it was hard enough taking time to see Boring Ray. I'm so busy with the farm that Erik and I being friends with benefits every other weekend sounds perfect right now." I stopped for a second, thinking of what new experiences could be on the horizon with Erik, the farm, or... who knows. "I just like the idea of saying 'yes' to whatever or really *who*ever may come along," I sighed.

"Why don't you want anyone finding out?" volleyed Skyler. I caught Sam looking over at her and smiling. The "Matchmaker" song came to my mind again, as I took a moment to answer. Maybe Skyler really could be the "cake" that brings Sam up here like she mentioned.

"It's no one's business really. I don't want to *have* to tell anyone. I told Larry about Ray and then he runs off and blabs it to Rosalie who tells *Erik*," I groaned. "Of course, I did tell a fifty-something year old man about my sex life. Not that y'all would, but I'd appreciate it if you didn't tell anyone."

Sam smiled, "Our lips are sealed. You think Erik will bring the fun, the energy and the foreplay?"

"Ooo... the trifecta?" I laughed. "I really have no idea. If that kiss on the front porch was any indication though, we should have a *real* good time."

"Could that be a song?" Sam grabbed the pepper grinder and jumped to her feet singing, "*Oh, oh, I'm lookin' for somebody to bang! Oh, oh, not anyone boring like Ray! Oh, oh... lookin' for somebody to bang! Oh, oh, Erik is hot, we need to quit being scared and bang!*" We danced to my new theme song adding verses up as we went that made no sense at all. My face hurt from laughing at our silliness.

We spent the rest of the afternoon watching Dateline reruns and finding out more about Skyler. Sam seemed smitten, so I didn't mind that she stayed all day... anything to entice Sam to make the move up here.

"What is this gala y'all are going to this weekend?" asked Sam, remembering what Erik had said before he left. Skyler had left after dinner, so Sam and I were enjoying a glass of wine in our pajamas on the deck.

"It's a charity event for the children's hospital. Erik and I donated a couple of guide packages with lodging, so we were invited to come," I smiled. "It'll be great exposure for the bed and breakfast and Erik's guide service."

"Look at y'all, working as a team already. I can't believe *you're* dressing up? Remember to take pictures. I have *got* to see this!" Sam laughed.

"I'll get pictures, I promise. I'll need evidence, I'm sure." I cozied up in my blanket in front of the fire and sipped my wine. Anxious but thrilling thoughts about this upcoming weekend whirled in my mind. My stomach hurt from laughing as I thought about Sam dancing around singing my new anthem. It was still in our head when I dropped her at the ferry terminal the next day.

"Love you, bitch," she moaned, grabbing her suitcase from my backseat.

"Love you! Remember that Skyler is just a plane ride away…," I cooed from the driver's seat.

"Have fun riding that dick this weekend!" she yelled after she shut the door.

I laughed, shaking my head as I turned the jeep towards home. Sam was exactly the distraction I had needed, but now I needed another one to get me to Saturday.

Chapter 17

I bounded out of bed and immediately put the electric kettle on to boil for my coffee. It was Saturday. The gala was tonight, and I was more than ready. *For the mind-blowing sex!* Nope, I had to clear my mind. The only communication between Erik and I was a text I sent earlier in the week reminding him of my schedule. He sent a thumbs-up emoji in response. *Maybe just some heavy making out.* I got dressed, put out breakfast in the lobby, and went out to start my morning chores. Larry was already feeding the chickens and smiled as I handed him a welcome cup of coffee.

"I'm leaving in a couple of hours for Seattle. You need anything before I go?" I asked him as we looked out over the yard.

"I just need for you to have a good time. Don't give us another thought," he said, sipping from his hot mug.

I gave him a sly smile as I replied, "I'll actually be thinkin' of y'all all night since it's publicity for this place."

"Good point!" he guffawed, nearly spilling his coffee. "Just promise me you'll let Erik show you a good time."

It was my turn to nearly spill my coffee. *What the fuck?* "What do you mean?"

Larry looked at me with confusion. "He *is* going to the party with you, right?" I nodded in response. "Well, you've been stuck around here so much since Jake passed, that I hope Erik shows you a good time in the city."

I smiled at Larry, realizing his remark was innocent. "I'm sure he will," I laughed as I turned and headed toward the barn. "But what happens in Seattle stays in Seattle!" I yelled and his raspy laughter echoed down the hill.

I finished my chores and made sure our current guests' needs were met. Our new full-time housekeeper was working out so well that I might actually get some free time soon. With my 'to-do' list cleared, I left the farm, turning the jeep east towards Seattle. My stomach was in knots with apprehension, happy that I was on my way to get pampered to help me relax for what might come.

I pulled into Erik's parking garage at exactly five o'clock, buffed and polished. It was such a relief to have professionals do my hair and makeup, plus I squeezed in a relaxing massage. My normal idea of dressing up was putting mascara on and calling it a day, so this was completely out of my wheelhouse. With my hair and makeup done to perfection, the only thing I had left to do was put on my dress. My stomach dropped as the elevator went up to Erik's floor. I had gone over scenarios in my head all week about how I would greet him after *the kiss*, but I decided I would just listen to Sam and go with Erik's flow. I had texted him that I was here when I pulled in, so he was waiting when the elevator opened.

"Hey... oh, wow," Eric breathed, taking in my hair and makeup, "You look great."

I brushed the shoulder of my flannel buttoned shirt and smiled, "Well, you said to dress fancy..."

He laughed as he extended his arm to welcome me inside, "Come on in. How much longer do you need to change?" We walked through a small entry into Erik's "flat". I had been there before a few times but only briefly, it wasn't often that I needed to come into the city. The vibe was masculine and modern with navy blue accents, wood tones, and towering ceilings that exposed the pipes and ducting.

"Fifteen minutes. Just need to change into something more comfortable," I smiled. *Too many jokes, Kelly.* Erik took my dress and overnight bag from my hands, goosebumps sprung up on my arms as our fingers touched.

"I'll be right back," he smirked, then took my bags down the hallway as I turned and began perusing the large, open room. From the windows in the corner, I could see

Puget Sound with the barges, ferries and sailboats floating by. Hard to believe that the farm was only a couple of hours away, when it felt like a million miles at the moment. I was out of my comfort zone, and it felt exciting… dressing up, the city… Erik. I could just make out the outline of mountains on the Peninsula in the distance when his voice broke my reverie. "Want to enjoy an adult beverage while I get dressed?" Erik was pulling out a stool at his oversized island and gesturing for me to sit. "Then you can use my room to dress, since the loo is bigger."

"I do like big loos," I laughed. "A cocktail would be lovely," I said sitting down. Erik started spinning a copper mug on his finger.

"Moscow Mule?" he grinned.

"My favorite."

"I know." I watched as he mixed the cocktail and grabbed a bowl of cut limes from the fridge. He brought the drink over but before setting it down, he raised the glass. "Cheers," he smirked, took a sip, and set it down in front of me.

"That's how germs are spread," I teased, looking up, meeting his gaze.

"Are you going to let me kiss you later?" he retorted, holding my stare with that panty-wetting smirk. *Holy fuck.*

"Good point," I sighed. Erik laughed all the way to his bedroom and shut the door. I grabbed my drink and wandered around studying his place. I made sure to drink from where his lips touched my glass. I couldn't help myself.

I zeroed in on all the framed pictures that were obviously Erik's family. Being the youngest of five in a close-knit family meant that there were a lot of them. I had met his three older brothers once before when he brought them out to the farm for a guide trip a few years ago. I remember them poking fun at him a lot, yet it was obvious they were proud of their youngest sibling. I even chimed in when they were ribbing him about his love life. *If they could only see me now...*

"Your turn, love."

Goosebumps sprang up on my arms again and my nipples stood at attention from the sound of that sexy voice behind me. I turned around and nearly dropped my empty glass. I had my very own James fucking Bond. Hair product was used to style Erik's dark locks to look like bed head perfection, his midnight blue suit fit like a glove, and he had left just enough scruff to be a sex dream come to life. I was speechless. *I'm going to fuck the shit out of him.*

"Or are you going to stand around and look at pictures all day?" he grinned with that panty-wetting smirk that made my vagina clench.

I finally found my voice. "Listen, double O seven... isn't that what the pictures are here for? To look at?" I smiled and took a quick breath. "You look... dashing."

"This old thing?" he teased, pretending to straighten his tie. He walked over and started looking at the same pictures I had been studying. "I once, *once,* told my family that it was best if they gave me framed pictures as gifts, so then I could just put them up. No fuss. I guess I should have put a limit on it," he laughed looking around at all the pictures smiling back at him.

"I think it's sweet. I bet it's hard to be so far away from them," I smiled up at him, and he smiled back but with a wicked glint in his eye. *What is he thinking?*

"It *is* hard," he smirked as I rolled my eyes, "Now go get dressed, so we can get this party started. We can have a drink together here then head over to the hotel bar to pre-game."

I curtsied with a wink and went to his bedroom to change. He had put my bag on his giant bed, so I grabbed my toiletry case from the top. I saw that my dress hung on the closet door, as I took a minute to take in my surroundings. Framed pictures were in here too… sprinkled around the room. I went to the bathroom that was still slightly humid from Erik's shower. His wet towel hung from the hook on the door and was still damp from when he used it. *Why not?* I leaned forward and breathed in the smell of his body wash that clung to the towel. *Good god in heaven.* I couldn't quite make out what the scent was, but I loved what it did to my insides. The real-life thing was waiting on me in the other room, so I got into gear. Wanting to check out his pictures later could get me back into his bedroom. *Genius!*

I dressed quickly, making sure I had just enough Spanx on to get me laid. I checked my reflection one last time. *Not too shabby.* My dress had one strap across my shoulder and was straight down with a slit up to my thigh, very flattering. Wedge shoes for the comfort win, and I was ready. I left my things as they were in Erik's bathroom (another reason to be back in here) and followed the classical music I heard toward the kitchen where another copper mug was waiting.

"Damn, you look... ravishing," Erik's voice melted my insides like butter.

"This old thing?" I smiled. "Thank you. It's fun to dress up every once in a while."

Erik smiled, placing his hand on my waist and pulled me close. The smell of his body wash from the towel filled my senses again. "I like it, but I prefer your cap and jeans," he murmured in my ear, making my eyes roll back in my head.

"You and me both," I squirmed. He led me over to an open stool, and we sat down to sip our drinks. I know we *had* to attend the gala, but I would have been perfectly fine sitting there with him for the night.

"How was the rest of Sam's holiday?" he asked, taking a sip of his drink.

"Uneventful really. We just stayed around the house and talked and talked and talked," I prattled as I made a talking motion with my hand.

"Shocker," Erik sighed sarcastically, making me roll my eyes. "How long did Miss Beer Rep stay?"

"*Skyler* left Sunday evening... I'm talkin' like eight o'clock! I thought about charging her for the night, but then I really would be a pimp... or would that make me a madam?" Erik shook his head at our shared joke.

We spent the next hour talking and laughing, deciding to stay there and drink for free rather than go early to the hotel bar where the gala was being held. The booze was starting to have the desired effect, so I visited the powder room one last time. I walked out to a rhythmic, up-tempo Latin beat that beckoned me back into the kitchen.

"Hel–lo, gorgeous," came that delicious voice from across the room. *So much for dry panties.* I turned around slowly, meeting Erik's eyes with my own as I wiggled my hips with the beat of the music. Smiling, I held his stare and started moving my arms like I was dancing a hula.

"Nice music. I love to dance," I murmured.

"I know."

Erik walked towards me, never looking away. He stopped just a couple of feet away from where I continued my dance to the hypnotic music.

"Are you going to dance with me?" I asked. Turning a circle then meeting his gaze again.

"I will at the gala but not now," he said gruffly.

"Why not now?" I asked innocently but ground my hips in a not-so-innocent way to the music.

Erik took another step forward so his body aligned with mine. I leaned into his heat. He placed both of his hands on my ass and pulled my hips to meet his, his erection evident as he ground his hips into mine and my breath hitched. He murmured in my ear, "Because if I dance with you *now*… we'll *never* make it to that bloody gala." Erik nipped at my earlobe before kissing my neck, then grabbed my hand and walked us to the elevator. *Thank you, baby Jesus for padded bras. My nipples could put someone's eye out right now.*

Minutes later, we were in the backseat of the rented town car slowly making our way through the streets of Seattle to the charity gala. The privacy screen was up between us and the driver, so we were in our own silent, little world.

"I brought this to ease the tension," Erik teased. I looked over and he was wagging a disposable vape pen like a cigar and wiggling his eyebrows.

"How can someone be so silly yet so sexy at the same time?" I asked. He laughed remembering the words. We each took a couple of drags and immediately I felt my shoulders relax. "I'd like a picture with you tonight. I like that we're all matchy-matchy," I said looking down at our ensembles.

"I heard you tell Sam that your dress was midnight blue, and I just happened to have this in my closet," he shrugged. "I didn't think we should clash."

"That was thoughtful of you."

"I'm not always a prick, love," he said, sending his sexy smirk in my direction.

"I've never actually seen your prick side, to be honest," I smiled.

His sexy smirk turned into a sexy grin as he leaned closer and murmured without breaking eye contact, "I plan on showing you that later tonight."

My eyes widened in surprise, but I didn't look away. Flecks of light from the city outside sparkled in his eyes as we stared at one another. *Fuck it.*

"I look forward to seeing that side of you," I murmured back.

Erik's brows shot up in surprise and he leaned over even closer. Running his hand up my thigh, he whispered in my ear, "That side wants to do many, *dirty* things to you." *Holy shit.*

His hand moved further up, but I squeezed my legs together before it reached its destination. "I would but… it's a little embarrassing," I sighed. *Not like I can hide it.*

"What, love?" Erik asked with concern, pulling his hand back.

"Oh, no no… it's nothing like that. I'm just a little… excited, so it's…" I really could have died from embarrassment, but I might as well get everything out in the open.

"Have I made you wet?" he groaned in my ear. I nodded. "Please, *God, please* let me feel, vixen." I hesitated then nodded again and his hand slid up my thigh. *Thank the Lord for crotchless Spanx.*

He slid a finger into my wet slit and his eyes grew huge. "*Fuuuuck,* Kelly! You are *so* wet. Did I do that to you?" he whispered and slid another finger in just once before pulling both out causing a mewling sound to escape my lips. I was unable to respond as Erik raised his two wet fingers and slowly pushed them into his mouth, sucking my wetness as he pulled them back out. "I knew you'd taste good," he moaned. I nearly came right then. Erik pulled my hand to the hard bulge in his pants. "Just so you know… this is what I'll be sporting all night because of you."

I rubbed my palm against him and squeezed lightly, causing a moan to rumble from his throat. I looked up to make sure he was okay, but his dark eyes burned with a fire I didn't recognize. "You are so incredibly sexy," he groaned as I traced his hardened manhood with my fingers. *I knew he'd have a big dick.*

I smiled, but the car slowing down made pulling my hand away seem like torture. "Right back atcha… but I think we're here," I sighed. Erik quickly adjusted his endowment while I checked my reflection in the mirror. A healthy blush now stained my cheeks, and I started to smile, when a sudden flash of panic flooded my mind. "Erik, I– I want you and I want this. But– but I don't want this to hurt our, our… friendship, in any way," I stammered, stumbling over my words as I hurried to get them out clearly.

He stared at me for a moment, almost as if he was memorizing my face before he whispered, "Then we won't let it, love."

"Friends… with benefits, then?" I asked, my eyes wide with anticipation.

Erik took a deep breath before replying, "If that's what you want…"

Nodding my head I answered, "It is… at least for now." I grabbed his hand, brought it to my lips, and kissed it softly trying not to smudge my lipstick.

He gave me his devilish smirk, but it seemed to be missing the usual twinkle in his warm, brown eyes. "For now, it is… mate," he teased. "Now let's go gala the fuck out of this place."

Elyse Rundell

Chapter 18

Though I was enjoying the lingering touches and
smoldering glances that Erik and I were sending each other
during the cocktail reception, I was almost regretting my
"friends with benefits" proclamation from the car. I was in
charm mode with my setting on full blast while we worked
the room, but I was afraid my wide blast was having
unintended consequences. Women, young and old (and
even a few men), were eyeing my date like he was a turkey
at Thanksgiving as we took pictures and mingled. I
reminded myself that he was coming home with me... or
rather me with him, so... there was no reason to be
jealous.

The dinner was surprisingly tasty. Erik and I laughed as we devoured our food, though I was unable to tell if it was actually good or just leftover effects of our pot-smoking in the car. The other guests at our table were not interested in group conversation, so Erik and I felt alone in a sea of high-priced tables.

"Was the food really good or am I still high?" I leaned over and asked in a hushed tone.

He leaned in, bringing us closer. "You're still high, but the bar is pretty low for food in these kinds of events," he chuckled.

"What's for dessert?" I asked, clapping my hands together and looking around the room to see if anyone was being served. Waitstaff were handing out plates with cups, but I was unable to make out what they contained.

"I know what I want," mumbled Erik, touching my bare shoulder and rubbing circles with his thumb.

"What's that?" I had been so distracted by dessert that I didn't notice Erik's hand until it touched my skin. Now he left a trail of fire wherever he touched. He leaned in even closer, placing his free hand on my cheek, gently guiding my head so he could whisper in my ear.

"Your pussy," he growled.

Sweet Jesus! I would have slid out of my chair if it wasn't for this Spanx. I had never been so turned on in a public place. Erik could have taken me right there on the table, and I would have excused it. Hell, half the people in this banquet hall would have excused us with the way he was wearing that suit.

I held up a finger and said loudly, "Check, please."

Erik pulled back laughing at me and the inquisitive expressions of our tablemates. We still had time left in the silent auction and dancing to get through before he could explore *that* particular dessert. Chocolate mousse was served and was the best course of the night. I smiled at Erik and slowly licked my spoon before placing it in my empty cup.

"Not bad, but I liked my idea better," he murmured in my ear.

"I did too," I murmured back. Erik closed his eyes and took a deep breath.

We finished our cocktails and grabbed another before we began milling around the silent auction items while the DJ began playing. I spied on our auction donations while Erik bid on a few items that piqued his interest.

"Ours are doing *so* well!" I gushed quietly, coming up next to him and grabbing his arm. He jumped slightly in surprise, catching me off guard. "Um… you were so right; this publicity is awesome. We may already book up completely for next season…" He still had not looked up. "Earth to Erik… You okay?" I started to look down at what item caught his eye, when he seemed to break free from his trance.

"That's brilliant, my love," he said, still sounding distracted. The DJ had started to play a smooth ballad, so he took my elbow and steered me toward the dance floor. "Let's dance."

Erik placed his hands on my waist and pulled me to him as I wrapped my arms around his neck and nuzzled close, swaying to the music. It was nice not knowing anyone here.

"Are you sure you're okay? You seemed distracted," I asked, looking up and meeting his sexy stare. He gave a lazy smile, and I saw the familiar twinkle in his eye had returned.

"Never better."

I smiled and moved my arms to his waist as we finished the song and danced on through the next similarly slow ballad. We parted when the tempo picked up and Erik went to find us another drink.

The rhythm of the dance floor was too much for me to ignore. Though I didn't mind standing out in a crowd, I was thankful for the motley crew of dancers that surrounded me. From white-haired elders to twenty-somethings, we all slowly combined until the dance floor was packed. I worried that Erik would lose me in the crowd, so I figured I'd stay in one place… that is, until lines formed for The Electric Slide and all bets were off. I moved with the crowd following the steps that turned us all around, laughing with those that were learning the steps. I caught Erik's eye from the edge of the dance floor where he held our drinks in the air and smiled. I danced my way through the crowd holding his stare while I bobbed and weaved. I stopped when I reached him and turned around giving a shimmy as I dipped and rubbed my ass up the front of his taut thighs. I glanced behind me with my own wicked smirk and turned to snatch my drink from his hand, taking a sip through the tiny straw. "Thank you," I mouthed.

Erik grabbed the tiny straw from his own drink, threw it on the ground, and slammed back the whole of its contents. He leaned down, his voice sounded hoarse as he growled in my ear. "Let's go, *now.*"

"Aye, aye captain." I saluted, then slammed my drink as he did, throwing the straw on the floor. He grinned as his fingers entwined mine and he pulled me from the crowd. No goodbyes were needed as we left, and our driver was waiting with the car thanks to Erik's fast texting skills. We were in the backseat barreling down the streets of Seattle in record time.

"Remind me to give him a good tip," Erik said as the privacy glass was lifting. The partition barely closed before his mouth collided with mine unable to bridle the desire that we both felt. My hands reached up and fisted his dark hair hardened by his hair gel pulling his mouth even harder to mine. Erik had wrapped his arms around me trying desperately to pull me closer. Our tongues explored one another and danced together while moans of need escaped my throat. I needed him closer. I reached down and lifted the slit of my dress over my hips. Pushing Erik against the seat, I flung my leg over and straddled his lap receiving a guttural groan from him in response.

"Fuuuck me..." he swore as we ground our hips together pulling down on my shoulders to bring us closer. I ran my fingers through his hair again, yanking just hard enough so he looked into my eyes.

"I'm trying..." I whispered, sending him into a laughing-coughing fit. "Sorry! Sorry!" I exclaimed, scrambling over and grabbing a bottle of water from the console and handing it to him. Erik grabbed the bottle and downed the entire thing, crunching the bottle up when it was empty. The coughing stopped and his breathing slowed.

"You gonna make it?" I asked with a chuckle.

He nodded. "I think so," and looked out the window as the car slowed. "Thank God, we're at the flat." Erik turned back around and brought his palm to my cheek. He leaned in and placed a light kiss on my swollen lips. "Let's get you upstairs."

Chapter 19

"Of course, the bloody lift would choose tonight to be slow," Erik grumbled, pulling me against him and kissing the back of my neck. Looking around quickly, I noticed we were the only ones in the lobby. I turned around and slid my arms under his jacket and around his waist, reaching up to plant kisses along his jawline.

"I'm sure it's all *<kiss>* most *<kiss>* here, *<kiss>*" I whispered. DING! We laughed as the elevator doors opened and Erik walked me in holding me close, since I was walking backwards. He punched the button for his floor and pushed me against the wall, crashing his mouth to mine that was just as demanding. I groaned as he pinned me to the wall to rub his covered, hardened manhood against my core. "Oh God, Erik!" I moaned loudly. He drew back enough to catch his breath and grin.

"I knew you'd be a screamer," he teased as we reached his floor. He took my hand and led me inside. The door closed and we came together again, devouring one another like there was no tomorrow. Erik's hand trailed down cupping my breast through the sheer fabric of my dress while I tried to push his jacket off his shoulders. Groaning, he pushed me back just enough so he could remove his jacket and throw it to the floor. I stepped forward and fumbled with the buttons of his dress shirt.

"Fuck it," he moaned, grabbing the front of his shirt and ripping the buttons apart.

He was beautiful. His body was designed by God himself... or maybe the Devil would be more accurate. I couldn't help myself... I stepped forward and touched his chest, running my hands lightly over every indention in wonder. I looked up to see him flash a teasing smile at my slow exploration.

"Do you like the view?" he taunted. I looked up and bit my lip.

"It'll do," I smirked.

"Ha! I'll show you exactly what it'll do," Erik laughed, grabbing my ass to lift me up and pin me against the wall as he did before. I slid down his bare torso as his hands slid up, hitching my dress up as he moved. He slid his palm down between our bodies and thrust two fingers deep inside my womanly middle.

"Fuck, fuck, fuck!" I yelled with each thrust of his hand. I bit down on the covered part of his shoulder where his open shirt still clung.

"Come for me, love… just like this," he demanded, as he thrust his fingers even faster. I thought my legs would give way as I shuttered when wave after wave of pleasure washed over me.

"Now wait, love, wait, wait just a moment," Erik begged, but I could barely move as the wave was starting to subside. He then set me down onto the back of his couch.

"Finally," he breathed, as he sheathed his cock in my warm center all the way to the hilt. *Fuck!*

We sounded like wild animals, our primal growls and moans rumbling from our throats as Erik pounded away and I met his thrust with my own hunger.

"Here I come," he groaned, still thrusting.

"Wait, wait a-a-a-AWWWW!" I wailed as I came again, the swells of pleasure left me gasping. Erik thrust twice more before his own loud moan bellowed from his lips and his body shuttered. We both fell to the floor in a heap, gasping for breath. I stared at the ceiling as my heart rate slowed. I brought my hands to my chest and started laughing.

"Not exactly the reaction I was expecting," Erik chuckled from his spot on the floor.

"I still have my clothes on," I sputtered, still laughing. I looked at Erik and laughed harder since his pants were still on just down around his ankles. He must have been unbuttoning them when he asked me to wait. From my vantage point, I couldn't quite see the weapon of lust that he had between his legs. I would have to make time for that later.

"Should we head on out to another club?" I teased.

Erik tilted his head up and smiled, setting it back down on the ground before he spoke. "You might want to check a mirror first, my love," he chuckled.

I picked myself up off the floor and offered a hand to Erik who waved it off chuckling louder. *Shit.* I hurried to the hall bathroom and flipped on the light. I squinted as my eyes grew accustomed to the bright light above the sink as I stared at my reflection in the mirror. *Double fucking shit!* My mascara had streaked down my face making myself look like a giant overdressed raccoon.

"So much for waterproof mascara!" I yelled as I walked down the hall to Erik's bathroom to wash up. I had just scrubbed the last of the raccoon mask from my face when Erik walked in and stood behind me at the sink, wearing a sexy smirk… and nothing else. I tried to turn for a better view, but he stopped me by kissing my neck right where the strap to my dress was connected.

"I've wanted to kiss you here for so long," he admitted. *So long?* But my thoughts were drowned out by the moans my mouth made as Erik reached around and massaged my breasts through my dress with his large, tanned hands. His eyes, holding my stare in the reflection in the mirror, were so erotic, I nearly came just standing there. He reached up to the strap on my dress and raised his eyebrows asking for permission. I nodded and swallowed the lump in my throat. I had never felt so exposed. Erik unbuttoned the strap letting it fall down above my breast. He kissed my skin where the strap had been, nipping it with his teeth.

My fingers ached to touch him, but he held me in place as he continued to remove my dress. A look of confusion crossed his face as he ran his fingers along my back. I lifted my arm revealing the zipper that held the dress in place and smiled at my tormentor. Erik reached up, entwining his fingers with mine, then slowly caressed my arm all the way down until he reached my underarm. He grasped my dress with one hand and drug the zipper down with the other letting it fall in a pool around my feet. My breath hitched when I saw my reflection in the mirror... like a wanton wench. My large breasts pushed up by the bustier were spilling out over the cups. Erik reached around and pulled the bustier down further to expose them both, my nipples hardened further in the cool air. His hands seemed even darker as he grasped my pale breasts and pushed them higher, rolling my nipples between his thumb and forefingers.

"Perfect," he breathed in my ear. I knew I was far from, but right there in that moment I believed him. "May I?" he asked, lowering his eyes to my bustier.

"Yes, *please*," I begged. He began to unhook the clasps but his expression in the mirror became worrisome the further he progressed. "What's wrong?" I asked, craning my neck to see behind me.

"This dodgy thing left marks on you," he grumbled as he rubbed my back where the clasps had reddened my skin.

"They'll go away after a while. It's supposed to be tight."

He muttered incoherently as he unclasped the remaining hooks with a cute, little scowl creasing his brow. Making the leap from sinful, sex god to caring cutie was quite a feat. I giggled at the thought. His eyes shot up with surprise and met mine again in the mirror.

"Are you giggling at me?" Erik's sexy smirk was back, and it had a direct link to my core. *Fucking Niagara Falls.*

"Maybe..." was all I could manage.

He turned me slowly around to face him, removing the bustier completely and threw it over his shoulder, while I shimmied out of my crotchless Spanx. His eyes bore into mine with a hunger that sent a shiver of desire down to my toes. Erik grasped both breasts, leaned down and teased my nipple with his tongue. He barely nipped my erect bud with his teeth, but it caused my whole body to shutter. With a groan, he captured my breast in his mouth, sucking and licking, massaging the other with his hand and pinching my nipple. I wracked my hands through his thick, dark hair and grabbed fistfuls to bring him closer. *Holy fuck.*

Erik pulled at my nipple with a slight nip as he released it and trailed kisses up my neck. *Heavenly torture.* He caressed my earlobe with his tongue, sucking it, then... I felt his hot breath on the same spot making it tingle from the change in temperature.

"Are you giggling now?" he murmured in my ear. My eyes widened in surprise. *Two can play that game.* I donned my sexiest smolder as I pushed Erik back a step, then leaned against the counter to take in the view... and what a view it was. Chiseled was the first word that popped into my brain. His shaft stood at attention beckoning me closer. I wanted to lick every last inch of him. Our eyes met again.

"We'll save the giggling for later," I said, stepping closer, maintaining our gaze. I reached up and touched his chest, dragging my hands down feeling every muscle and movement. I leaned down and flicked his nipple with my tongue. Taking it in my mouth, I performed the same dance he had done with mine, heating it with my breath at the end making him shutter. I kissed down his rippled belly and kneeled down using my dress on the floor as a cushion. I wasn't normally one to think that a man's cock was anything of beauty, but Erik proved me wrong. It was gorgeous. I reached out and grasped his length in my hand. He groaned as I kissed the head of his shaft and licked the underside. I loved the feeling of power that giving head gave me. I looked up innocently as I took his head in my mouth again, met his gaze… and gave him a sly wink. He moaned, and I took him in deeper then, pulling him out to rub my tongue over his head.

"Oh, God!" he hissed as I took him in deeper. He had girth and length, but luckily, I had a big mouth. Erik pulled at the bobby pins in my hair trying to grasp a handful to hold. I continued taking him in and out of my mouth, sucking as I did, using my hand at the base of his shaft to help with his length.

"Fuck! Yes… here I come, here I come," he gasped trying to pull himself back. I pushed back, pulling him in deeper, feeling the come, warm in my throat as I swallowed. *His jizz isn't even that bad.* "You are so bloody sexy," Erik groaned as he helped me to my feet. He placed his hands around my neck and pulled me forward into a deep kiss. My insides immediately reignited as my tongue danced with his.

"It's like I've been starving," he murmured, pulling back, feathering kisses around my mouth, "and you're the first bite of food," he finished biting my lower lip and sucked it gently. I moaned as he slid his tongue in and out and fucked my mouth with it.

"I'm ready for the rest of my dessert," he grinned and kissed my neck.

Chapter 20

"Dessert?" I asked. Realization dawned when I saw Erik's wicked smirk and lustful eyes. *My pussy.* My eyes widened. I ached to have his mouth on my most sensitive area, but I needed a shower first. He must have sensed my hesitation.

"Are you a dirty girl?" he whispered in my ear. I nodded.

"I blame you." *Don't chicken out, Kelly.*

"Me?" he asked, feigning innocence. "What did I do?"

I took a breath and whispered in my most sultry tone, "You've kept my pussy wet all day."

Erik's eyebrows shot up in surprise and his eyes darkened with arousal. *Bingo.* He spun me around to face the counter, clutched my breast with one hand and started sliding his other down my belly. His eyes met mine reflected in the mirror. *So fucking hot.*

"I've kept this poor pussy wet all day?" He kept massaging my breast while his other hand ventured further down. A sound of agreement was all I could muster as I watched his hand descend.

"Does it need attention?" His fingers were hovering over my feminine lips, teasing the opening. My hips bucked forward. "Is that a yes?"

"*Please,*" I whined. I needed relief. He plunged two fingers deep inside my core.

"Is *that* what you want?" he growled into my ear as he tickled my sex watching me come undone in the mirror. I could only throw back my head in ecstasy as I felt the shudder of an orgasm building. I shuddered again when Erik pulled out his fingers causing me to cry out.

"I'm sorry, love, but I've got to feel you," he said hoarsely, I turned to face him, and he pushed me up onto the counter. We kissed as he moved between my legs and pushed the tip of his beautiful manhood into my opening. He hissed as he slowly slid in. I wrapped my legs around his waist to pull him closer.

"This won't take long," Erik grinned as he backed his cock out slightly just to slam it back into the hilt.

"Awww!" I sang, as I squeezed my legs tighter and rode that dick as he fucked me for all we were worth. My orgasm vibrated throughout my body as Erik poured himself into me letting out a grunt of satisfaction.

"Fuuuuck…" he moaned into my lips as I gasped when he pulled out. "Told you it wouldn't take long," he grinned, making me laugh with his cocky attitude. *And he earned every bit of that attitude.*

"Now I *really* need a shower."

Erik bent down and nuzzled the side of my neck with his nose and licked me all the way up to my earlobe. "You're right… too salty," he whispered. I laughed and spanked his bare, sexy ass. *Damn.* "I'll give you some space," he smiled.

The warm water from the showerhead melted all my little aches away. Erik's shower was huge (*like his dick… Stop it, Kelly!*) and part of me wanted some company, but the older, wiser part of me was tired and needed some rest. I heard music start in the bedroom, but it was too hard to hear with the noise of the shower.

"Do you mind turning that up?" I said loudly. Erik opened the bathroom door about a foot and the up-tempo beat of the music wafted in.

"Better?"

"Yes, thank you," I sang while already swaying my hips with the beat of the music. It was a fun pop song that I had heard a couple of times but hadn't quite figured out the words. I danced my way through the remainder of my shower while some of my favorite songs played. *What a fun channel.* I had just turned off the shower when movement caught my eye through the open bathroom door. Erik was lying on the bed watching me, smirking that delicious smirk. I rolled my eyes and flipped him the bird with both hands. His eyebrows shot up and he leaped from the bed.

"Wait! That wasn't an invitation!" I shrieked, laughing as he came in, grabbed a towel off the hook and playfully yanked me out of the shower.

"Don't worry. I'm knackered, darling," he soothed, drying me off with the towel. "Want to get high and lie in bed?"

"You know me so well," I beamed.

We laid in bed talking late into the night. He spoke of his family in England and the ups and downs of being a "whoopsy" baby (his next older sibling was just a little younger than me.) His father had passed away when he was young (we had that in common), and his mother was his hero. I spoke of my kids who were each doing well in their lives and my family and friends in Texas. We spoke of our respective businesses and their futures and fell asleep with the morning sun just starting to peek through the clouds.

Erik woke me the next morning partaking in his "dessert" from the night before. *What a wakeup call!* After an earth-shattering orgasm from his delightfully, wicked tongue, we fucked until we both collapsed falling asleep tangled in each other's arms.

It was just after noon when we began to stir.

"I'm starving," Erik mumbled, then blew a raspberry on my stomach where he was resting his head. I giggled and pretended to push his head lower, but yanked at his hair to pull him back up when he seemed all too eager to comply. My vagina needed a break.

We decided on a close, casual brunch spot, so I borrowed a cap from the stack in Erik's closet instead of trying to make any sense of my hair. Hand-in-hand, we walked down the busy, Seattle street to the cafe and snagged a table on the patio to enjoy the beautiful weather. Our first round of bloody marys came and went before we even ordered our food. I hesitated and looked at the time when the server asked if we wanted another round, but Erik went ahead and ordered.

"Will you stay one more night?" he asked when we were alone.

"That could be fun," I smiled. The thought had already crossed my mind, since Erik often stayed over on Sunday nights due to the heavy traffic going back to the city. A few texts and schedule confirmations later, I was cleared for one more night.

"Rosalie is going to cover for me," I said, finishing up my last text to Larry and taking a nice long drink of my cocktail. "She said she wants details of your dick as payment," I laughed.

"And what details might you share?" Erik asked, leaning forward with a devilish glint in his narrowed eyes. He reached over and swiped his finger in the hollandaise sauce of my eggs benedict. I grabbed his hand and licked the sauce from his finger, sucking the end and nipping it with my teeth.

"I don't kiss and tell," I winked.

I could see Erik's eyes start to dilate with desire as he leaned in even closer and murmured in my ear, "I wish I could lay you across this table, pull your panties down, and tongue-fuck your soaking wet pussy until you beg me to stop." He then leaned back in his chair and motioned to the server for another round of drinks. *Soaking wet pussy was right.*

My mouth hung open in a mix of shock and delight. Erik feigned innocence and asked loudly, "Are you alright, love?" unable to hold a straight face for long.

"Bastard," I said and took another drink.

Conversation flowed as nicely as the drinks for the remainder of the afternoon, until the side eyes of the waitstaff for our incredibly long brunch caught our attention.

"I think we better move along... plus I believe I've been over served," said Erik, in an attempt at a whisper. A group of giggling young women a couple of tables over made it known that he failed. He tipped an imaginary hat at their table as we walked by, eliciting another round of high-pitched giggles that made me cringe... it didn't help that I had been "over served" as well.

"C'mon, Casanova. We'll walk it off on the way back home," I pushed him towards the door trying not to stumble. We leisurely walked a meandering path back to Erik's flat, stopping at window displays, and peeking in shops that caught our interest. We passed Pike Place Market and saw all the displays of colorful flower bouquets. Erik slung his arm across my shoulders, pulling me close and kissed my head.

"This is where I always buy your flowers. I swing by here on my morning runs and grab a bouquet before making the drive." We walked through the crowded market, and Erik waved to one of the flower vendors, a short, dark-haired woman giving him a toothy grin. He grabbed two identical bouquets, paid, and told her he would see her later this week. I wasn't sure if she spoke English, since she never said a word, but her smile said it all.

"Why two... bouquets?" I asked. A look of confusion crossed Erik's face before he spoke.

"I... I guess I thought that you'd leave one here and take one with you... maybe. Then, this week, I could look at them and think of you and, and you know... whatever," he shrugged and shook his head. "Am I a bloody sap, or what?"

"You *are,* Casanova... We'll blame the alcohol," I said smiling. I wished I could blame the alcohol for the backflips my stomach was performing at the moment, but I knew better. Friends with benefits was off to a fantastic start.

The flowers were forgotten until the next morning, when I picked them off of the floor and propped them in the sink. Who knew it was so hard to hold on to a bouquet of flowers when you're drunk and getting fucked on the floor in the entryway? Finding a water pitcher, I arranged one of the bouquets for Erik's place as a final touch, since I was packed and ready to head back to the farm. I stood in the doorway of his bedroom for a moment watching him sleep, wondering if I would ever have dry panties again. His tousled dark hair fell against the pillow and his arms were stretched out over his head. Erik's dark eyelashes fluttered, and he opened his eyes, slowly taking in his surroundings. He smiled lazily when he saw me standing there watching.

"Good morning, vixen. What are you doing standing all the way over there?" he yawned. I returned his smile and walked over, leaned down and kissed him, sliding my tongue across his lips and nipping at the bottom one.

"Good morning, sleeping beauty. I'm afraid I have to go." Erik grabbed my face with both hands and brought me in for a deeper, longer kiss.

"Rubbish. Take your clothes off and get back in my bed," he smirked, slapping my ass. His bare chest was almost too much of a temptation to walk away from.

"*Very* tempting, but I really do have to go. Checkout at the farm is at eleven, and the rooms won't clean themselves," I sighed, rubbed my hand over his chest and lightly twisted his nipple, making him grin.

"Technically, they *will* since you hired the new housekeeper," he reminded, his wicked grin growing larger. "So climb up on this dick, you wanton woman!" he yelled, throwing back the sheets and pulling me down on top of his gorgeous, naked body. Shaking with laughter, I kissed him loud on the mouth and sat back up.

"You have no idea how much I want to, but I really do have to go. The new housekeeper is not fully trained yet. I'm sure the next couple of weeks will fly by," I said, standing up and grabbing my bag. Erik propped his arms up behind his head and gave me a lazy, half smile.

"Next couple of weeks? You mean next few days, love. I'll be at your place this weekend, remember? This weekend was the gala, not a guide weekend."

"You mean you get to see me three weekends in a row?" I threw a pillow at his sexy head. "Someone might be getting a little spoiled." Erik laughed and stood up, gloriously naked, wrapping his arms around me in a bear hug.

"Don't fret. We'll be back to every other weekend soon enough. You'll just have to endure extra benefits for a little while longer, my friend," giving me one last sexy smirk for the road.

Elyse Rundell

Chapter 21

Rosalie asked about Erik's dick twice that week, and I never confirmed or denied. I could tell that she was not happy with the lack of detail, but it was fun keeping her on her toes. It was Thursday night, and I was sitting under the awning on the outdoor sofa due to the steady drizzle of rain that was falling. I had wished that Erik would have come out tonight but plans in the city kept him there until tomorrow. Starting the fireplace, I curled up under a blanket and began to soak in the cool, night air when my phone buzzed with a notification.

Smiling, I read the text message, "You up?" from Erik. I sent him back a GIF that read "Duh!" It was only a little after eight... Plus, taunting him was so much fun. I held my phone waiting for his reply when it rang, making me jump and nearly drop it in the fire. I fumbled and was finally able to answer.

"H– Hey. Hey!" I stammered.

"Hey…" Erik responded, sounding suspicious, "Are you being naughty?"

I laughed. "Not just yet. What are *you* doing?" *Please say being naughty.*

"I'm on my way to see *you*, in fact. Hope you don't mind." I could tell he was smirking even through the phone.

"I don't mind at all." The butterflies in my stomach were doing somersaults. "Did your dinner plans fall through?"

"Fortunately, they did. Besides, I'd rather come *on* you… I mean come *with* you… I mean come *SEE* you. Sorry," he teased, making me laugh out loud.

"I'm out on the deck, so just come on back when you get here. Be careful!"

"I will, love. Be there in a jif." I jumped up off my comfy spot on the sofa to complete some grooming maintenance for the night of shameless fuckery I was anticipating. I was back on the couch trying to keep panty-wetting thoughts away when I heard the chime announcing someone on the driveway. I grabbed my phone and readied my music for his arrival. I heard the side gate open and pushed play. "Pony" by Ginuwine started playing lightly through the speakers. Erik chuckled when he heard the music.

"You hoping for a show, vixen?" he asked, cocking an eyebrow as he sauntered towards me. I gave him my most inviting smile.

"Always, darlin'." He was a fantastic dancer when he was in the mood, and I was hoping that he would be.

Erik dropped his bag on a chair, took off his shirt, and threw it at my head with a sly smile. He began thrusting his pelvis with the music as he ran his hand down his toned abdomen and grabbed his cock through his jeans. *Hot damn, my very own strip show.* I had been expecting him to dance, but not a full-on lap dance. He started to fall forward toward me on the couch then caught himself on the arm and did a push up as he kissed me deep on the lips. Erik pushed himself up and grabbed my hips, pulling me across his lap. I straddled him while he still thrust against me with the music, our mouths demanding more and more from one another. *So fucking hot.* I squirmed against him begging for relief from the ache I already felt below.

"You little vixen," his voice slightly hoarse, "are you not wearing any panties?" I had changed from my T-shirt and pajama pants to a sundress when he called despite the cold.

"I thought I would save us some time," I murmured in his ear, licking his earlobe and biting it gently.

"I've got to taste you," Erik growled, rolling me over so that he was on top. The music be damned at this point. He nibbled down my body quickly and nuzzled my bare lips with his nose breathing in my womanly scent.

"I've dreamt of this all week," he moaned as he licked my heated center and slid his tongue over my clit.

My hips bucked up begging for more as I grabbed handfuls of his hair to pull him closer.

"Fuuuck…" I gasped, my eyes rolling back in my head as I came all over his tongue. He moaned, sucking my juices from my climax as he tickled his tongue against my center. Erik sat up quickly, yanking his pants down, he pulled out his hard cock and pressed it to my opening.

"Tell me you want me," he groaned into my ear.

"Oh God! I want you," I moaned, wrapping my legs around his waist, I pushed up against his massive erection.

"Is this what you want?" he asked, pressing into me further. I could hardly breathe.

"Yes!" I gasped, pushing against him more.

Erik grabbed my ass with one hand as he rammed his cock into my warm, welcoming core. My eyes rolled back as his other hand reached between us to finger my throbbing sex while he thrust in and out. It was almost more than I could bear.

"FUCK!" he shouted, and it echoed across the small valley around us as he came, still thrusting until I clenched my vaginal walls, coming around his beautiful dick. *Holy shit!*

Erik and I spent the rest of the night catching each other up on our week and ended up falling asleep outside, wrapped in the blanket on the outdoor couch. We woke when the sun made its debut the next morning. Erik set off on his guide trip with our plans in place for the next night while I met Larry in the barn to start our day.

It was nearly seven o'clock the next evening when Larry pulled up with Erik and his Assholes. Apparently, there had been some obstructions along the trail and detours were necessary to get back. I locked eyes with Erik as they disembarked the transport van. It took every bit of self-control I could muster not to run and throw myself against him. He smiled and winked, as Larry gave them instructions for the rest of the evening. I had smoked a brisket all day and had all the fixin's prepared, so the Assholes would get cleaned up and meet back at the big house for dinner.

"Hope you're not too tired," I nudged Erik's shoulder as we turned toward the house. "Did you have a nice ride?" I was trying my best to act normal since Larry was within hearing distance.

"We did. This was a fast group, so we got further than I planned. How was your day?" Erik asked, and I could tell he was trying for normal as well. Before I could reply, Larry yelled for me needing a hand unhooking the rig.

"It was good. I'll see you in a little while," I smiled motioning back at Larry. Erik smiled and headed inside.

"This looks fantastic," cooed Mike, one of Erik's regular Assholes when we were gathered for dinner. The food was set buffet-style out on the deck and almost all the Assholes were back from getting cleaned up after their ride. Everyone was milling around, enjoying the cool weather and the open bar.

"I can tell you can handle some meat," said another of the Assholes, underneath his breath as he walked up beside me. I didn't recognize him, but from the vulgar way he was looking at me, I was fine with that. I glanced around for Erik, but he still must have been upstairs cleaning up. I had hoped I would find him in my shower when I ducked my head in after I helped Larry, but no such luck.

"We haven't formally met," said the unknown Asshole who was still staring at me, "I'm Damon. What's your name? Cause I've been calling you sexy since I saw you," he leered. I thought I might vomit but smiled politely. His dark brown eyes seem to lack something... maybe a soul. Creepy was the first word that came to mind. I glanced around, but the other Assholes didn't seem to notice his behavior.

"I'm Kelly. Hope y'all had a good ride today," I turned toward the group to include them in my statement. Everyone nodded and mumbled in agreement as they filled their plates... everyone except Damon.

"I did have a good ride," he grinned nastily, "I'll be looking for a different kind of good ride later," he mumbled, laughing and gyrating his hips. *Did he think this was attractive?*

I ignored the crass comment and went to the kitchen to remove myself from the toxicity... too bad it followed me in.

"You didn't like my joke?" Damon asked. He had walked up and was standing next to me by the sink. A shudder of disgust came over me, but I had to remind myself that this was *my* house... plus, everyone was just outside.

"I didn't realize you had made one," I replied stoically, and started putting the dirty dishes into the dishwasher hoping he would lose interest.

"You must be lonely these days," he suggested with his weasley voice, taking a step closer and touching my arm, "so let me know if you need any help with that." I thought I was going to be sick.

"I'm good, you should probably step back," I said, taking a deep breath trying to swallow the bile in my throat.

"Get the *fuck* away from her, *mate*," came a low, menacing voice from the bottom of the stairs. Damon immediately jumped back a good two feet when he heard Erik's voice. "Get to your cabin and if I see you even *look* at her, I will fuck your shit, do you understand?" Erik asked with his voice quavering, trying to remain calm. He took a few more steps into the kitchen.

"Sorry, man. It's cool. We're cool. I'll just grab a plate and head out," Damon sniveled, walking backwards and did not turn around until he was by the door and walked out. Erik took a deep breath before walking to me. He slid his hand to my cheek and looked earnestly into my eyes.

"Did he do anything to you?"

"No, just some lewd comments that are probably par for the course with him. I think you probably scared the shit out of him."

"Good, that was the point," he whispered, smoothing my hair behind my ear. We stood like that for a moment, the low sounds of conversation from the deck were the only sound in the room. He looked around to make sure we were still alone before lightly kissing my mouth, smiling and heading outside. I smiled as I touched my lips where Erik's had just been. I'm sure I could have handled Damon the Creeper on my own, but being a damsel in distress with Erik as my brave knight was a fantasy I could get behind.

The remainder of the evening had been a success, with no one even mentioning Damon the Creeper's sudden departure. Erik did seem distracted, but I chalked that up to the confrontation with the Creeper.

Larry and Rosalie were the last to leave, as usual. I walked them to the door to say goodnight and locked it behind them, took a breath, then walked back into the kitchen.

"Kel–ly," Erik called from the back deck.

"Er–ik," I called back as I walked out the open sliding door. He was lying on our lounge chair with his arms open wide in invitation. I grinned as I threw my leg over and sat down facing him. Erik leaned up, wrapped his arms around me bringing me closer as I touched his face and kissed him passionately.

"I take it we're finally alone," he mumbled as I kissed along his jawline.

"Uh huh," was all I got out as I kissed his delicious mouth again, plunging my tongue in to touch and taste his.

"I've been wanting to do this since I got out of that van tonight," he groaned as he kissed down my neck.

"Me too," I whimpered as Erik palmed my breast over my shirt, "But let's clean up first *then* we can play as long as we want," I murmured in his ear, my voice deeper from desire.

"Vixen..." he sighed as he helped me up. We finished cleaning in a hurry, finding ways to brush up against each other here and there as we worked.

"So how do you know Damon the Creeper?" I asked as Erik came over and stood by me at the kitchen island. We had finished cleaning in record time.

"The Creeper?" Erik chuckled. "Seems fitting. I apologize for his behavior. He's just an arsehole that would ride with me when I first moved to Seattle, but we fell out of touch. Now I remember why."

"It's fine. You saved him from getting kneed in the balls," I smiled.

Erik returned with his own tender smile, "I have no doubt you could have taken him. I just saw red when I came down the stairs and saw him so close to you."

I kissed him lightly on the lips. "Thanks for being my knight in shining armor," I smiled, and he kissed me lightly back. "I know it's not sexy..." I looked up at him as he eyed me cautiously, "but we need to talk about parameters. Friends with benefits rules."

"Can we call it something better... like fuck buddies?" he grinned.

"Sure," I smiled, "Fuck buddy rules."

"That sounds much better. Now go on with your rules, fuck buddy," he teased. I rolled my eyes and tried to stay serious.

"First, I want to keep this between us."

"So no threesomes."

I looked up and laughed, "No threesomes, but I was meaning I don't want anyone to know about us. It's no one else's business, you know?"

"Got it. Our little secret... but what about when it's just the two of us?" he asked, pushing back some strands of hair that had fallen out of my messy bun.

"What about it?" I murmured, leaning into his touch as he brushed my face with the back of his hand.

"Can I kiss you whenever I want?" he whispered, inching closer, looking down at my mouth. I nodded as he gently touched my lips with his for just a moment before pulling back. "Nice... what's your next rule?"

"Not necessarily a rule, but... I think we should see other people... when we're not together, of course," I stumbled. "And use condoms if you do, because I don't want to use them with you." I took a breath since I rushed out my last statement. I looked up at him to gauge his reaction, when I remembered, "And I don't want to know if you do," I mumbled looking down at the emblem on his shirt, waiting for his response.

"You'll see other people too?" he asked. I looked up at him in surprise by the tone of his voice.

"I would. Not that I would seek anyone out or whatever, just if I'm asked and I'm interested," I said softly.

Erik thought for a moment before responding, "Let me know if anything gets serious."

"It won't," I reassured. His eyes narrowed as he seemed to be contemplating my reply.

"What makes you so sure?" he asked earnestly. The sweet look in his brown eyes was enough to make my heart melt.

I gave him my sweetest smile in return. "Because if I was going to be serious with anyone, I would want it to be you."

Erik's eyes darkened as he lifted my ass on to the counter. He settled between my thighs as our mouths joined, mine hard and demanding, his slow and seductive. I pulled back, surprised at his change in technique. I slid my hands down his torso and began unfastening his jeans. Erik stopped my progression by moving my hands and placing them around his neck and continued his slow torture by kissing my neck and caressing my skin under the back of my shirt. I slid my hands up his neck and grabbed fistfuls of his hair as I encouraged him to take the kissing lower. Erik chuckled, loosening my grip on his hair and brought my hands back down to his neck. He began kissing my neck again, starting the seduction all over. Every time I tried to go further, he would stop me and begin again.

"You make me want to scream," I growled, when he stopped me yet again.

"There's my dirty girl," he grinned. "What's the rush?" I rolled my eyes in response. "Patience, love, patience," he whispered in my ear as he picked me up off the counter. I yelped and locked my legs around his waist.

"This cannot be good for your back! Put me down!" I squealed. He laughed and hitched me up higher.

"You let me worry about my back, I'm taking you to bed," he grumbled into my neck as he bit me.

"Does this mean you agree to the rules?" I yelped.

"For now," he smiled. Erik stopped at the side of my bed and slowly slid me down his body until I was sitting on the edge. He took a step back and stopped, looking around the room. A look flashed across his face that I couldn't read.

"Hey, hey… what's the matter?" I grabbed his hand and pulled him toward me, and he sat down on the bed beside me. "Hey…talk to me," I soothed and kissed the side of his head.

Erik took a deep breath but remained silent as the quietness swirled around us. He took another deep breath then began to speak. "It's like I need to show Jake some respect while I'm bedding his woman," he sighed, looking down at our entangled hands.

"You've 'bedded' me already, Erik," I contended, kissing the corner of his mouth. "But feel free to *dis*respect me all you want," I murmured, licking his bottom lip.

He let out a groan, kissed me back deeply, then pulled back again raking his hands through his thick hair. "Not in this bed, I haven't," he sighed letting out another deep breath.

I glanced around the room and tried to envision what the room looked like through Erik's eyes. I immediately looked at the framed pictures sprinkled around the room and remembered the vast number of pictures that Erik had of his family.

"Would it help if I moved the pictures?" I offered. He glanced around the room and smiled back at me.

"Not right this second, but it would be nice not to have my mate smiling at me while I'm shagging his wife," he chuckled.

I let out the pent-up breath I was holding. "I'm just happy you want to shag me," I laughed a little too nervously. Realization flashed across his face. He moved swiftly, pulling me up against him then rolling me over so he lay on top of me.

"That was *never* the issue, love," he hissed as he ground his erection into my hip.

"Then what is it?" I asked timidly, nuzzling my face into his neck.

"It's like I want to show him that I'm worthy… to have you," he tipped my chin back, so I could look into his eyes. "At least the first time in this bed that you shared… I want to worship you," he kissed me softly, dipping his tongue in and touching mine lightly before pulling it out, "Make love to you," he murmured, kissing me again but deeper. *Oh my.* I moaned in encouragement as I slowly met his tongue with mine and caressed it, taking the time to explore his mouth. Erik ran his hands down my body and back up slowly taking my shirt with him as he grazed my skin. I had already removed my bra when the others had left, so my chest was his for the taking. I did feel worshiped as he caressed my breasts, teased my nipples with his tongue and finally bit gently as he took turns pulling each one into his mouth. This was so different from our normal frenzied fuckery, but there was a slow burn starting to build down below that was just as delicious.

I gently ran my hands up Erik's torso mimicking how he lifted my shirt. I sat up to push it over his head, rolled over and straddled his waist. It was my turn to worship at the altar of Erik. My hands glided over his rippled torso, while I rocked my pelvis against the hard bulge in his jeans. He groaned as I bent down and kissed along his chest, teasing his nipple with my tongue, biting it as he had done to me... then tormented his other side as well. He pushed his hips into mine with more force.

"This is harder than I thought," he moaned, bucking his hips when I reached for the button of his jeans.

"That's what she said," I murmured, sliding his zipper down. He grinned and let out a loud "yes" as I stroked his manhood still shielded by his boxer briefs. Needing to be freed, Erik rolled me over kicking free of his jeans and underwear. He grappled with my jeans, until he was finally able to pull them off along with my underwear, then nestled his hips between mine and nudged my entrance with his rock, hard staff.

"I thought we were going slow," I smiled, as Erik opened his mouth wide and suckled my breast, making me gasp. My hips thrust forward involuntarily begging to be filled.

"No one said slow, love, just worthy," he moaned, as he gently entered me completely. He pulled back then entered again while circling his hips that made me groan in ecstasy. *Holy fuck, could he move.* We kept this steady pace and I felt myself quickening, building... needing more friction to fall over the edge. Erik must have sensed it as he increased the force, gliding into me over and over.

He moaned in my ear, "But I'm going to fuck you like a dirty little slut later."

"FUCK!" I screamed, falling over the edge with a climax for the record books. Wave after wave crashed over me, as I heard Erik's cries of ecstasy as he emptied into me. We laid there for a while letting our breathing steady, unable to move. Erik was the first to break the silence with his chuckling.

"You love it when I talk dirty," he grinned, tracing his finger along my jawline.

"Don't think I can deny that," I smiled, turning to look at him. "Mission accomplished. I feel thoroughly worshiped."

I still felt worshiped as he fucked me like a dirty, little slut the next morning. Good thing for good insulation or our whole farm would have received an early morning wakeup call when I screamed Erik's name as he pounded into me.

We enjoyed our coffee naked in bed since it was so early. Breakfast was always later on Sundays, allowing myself a day to sleep in.

"Why do you want us to date other people?" asked Erik, glancing over at me as he took a sip from his mug. *Real talk for early in the morning.*

"I'm not ready for a full-time relationship, and I don't want to hold you back from finding someone that could make you happy," I smiled and shrugged.

"What if *you're* the one that makes me happy?" he asked candidly.

I smiled and kissed him, running my tongue along his coffee-tinged lips. "We'll give it time and see what happens."

"The age difference doesn't bother *you*, does it?" he asked sincerely, looking into my eyes as he asked.

"Not really. I usually forget about it when we're together. I don't doubt that other people might have a

191

problem," I rolled my eyes. "Be honest… Does it bother you at *all*?"

"Not at all. Honestly. My mum has always said I was an old soul, but that's probably because my siblings were all so much older than me," he smiled, putting his mug down on the nightstand. He touched my face with both his hands. "Your age is one of the things I love about you, Kelly. It brings a confidence that is hard to find in younger women," he shared then drew me in for a soft kiss.

"Mission accomplished," I murmured against his lips and smiled.

Chapter 22

A couple of months had gone by and my "fuck buddy" relationship with Erik was exactly what I had hoped. We saw each other every other weekend without fail, and it was always hard to see him leave. I told Erik the anticipation must make sex hotter, since our appetite for each other had only increased.

I was daydreaming about that appetite instead of making the guest bed, when my phone rang one sunshiny morning. It was Sam! She and I had been playing phone tag for a while, so we needed to catch up.

"Finally!" I answered in greeting.

"Right? It's been forever. Did I catch you in the middle of anything?"

"Just tonguing Erik's asshole," I said laughing. It was nice to have one person I could talk to about Erik.

"I do hope you don't mean literally, you dirty bitch!" she shrieked. "Is the sex still phenomenal?" she asked.

"As good as you think it could be, times ten," I cooed as I flopped down onto the bed.

We caught each other up. Kids (mine and hers) and grandkids (hers) were good. Skyler had been down *twice* to see her! *Say what!?* I filled her in on my life... and Erik.

"So has he banged anyone else?" she inquired offhandedly.

"I told him not to tell me, but I don't think so," I thought about it for half a second. "You know, I have no idea if he has. I just told him to use protection if he did. I try not to think about it."

"Out of sight, out of mind, kinda thing?" she laughed. "Ooo Lord, you would not want to deal with any dang STDs at our age," she added.

"Exactly! I already had a UTI when we first got together, that was bad enough. I guess that's what happens when you have to dust out the cobwebs," I laughed. "He seems happy, I'm happy, business is booming... besides missing Jake sometimes so bad it hurts... I can't complain," I sighed. "Oh! I nearly forgot to tell you. Lindsey, Ash, and Diane are coming in today for a long weekend."

"Dang it. Too bad I can't make it. Shoot," moaned Sam, dripping with sarcasm. She had never been a fan of my college girlfriends, and the feeling was mutual... especially after Sam "turned into a dang lesbo" as Diane put it. "Hold up! Are you going to introduce them to Erik? Maybe I *do* want to come!" she shrieked.

"What? As my fuck buddy? Yeah right! They'll meet him Saturday night for sure when he gets back from his guide trip. Larry is doing another crab boil for us. They all met Erik at Jake's funeral, and Lindsey met him that one infamous weekend. I plan on keeping it normal, or at least making it look like things are normal." I wasn't sure if Erik was ready yet to be thrown to the lions, or lionesses as they were.

"Just rip the band aid off and tell them first thing. Maybe they'll have grown tired of the crib-robbing jokes by the time Saturday rolls around," she cackled.

"No thank you," I said, "though I can't imagine that they'd ever get tired of poking fun at me. I'll let you know what happens." My girls did love to make jokes, and I was usually an easy target. My hijinks in college were legendary and still gave them ammo to this day. I was sure that my relationship with Erik would be added to their war chest if they found out.

I finished straightening the rooms for my guests to arrive once Sam and I hung up. My friends had rented a car at the airport, so it was nice not having to make a trip to get them. I hadn't seen Ash and Diane since Jake's funeral and Lindsey only once, so I was looking forward to our visit... though constructing a plan to keep Erik and my relationship low key plagued my mind. I don't really know what their reaction would be, if they found out. I anticipated some judgment and the third degree about our age difference, but nothing that would change my mind about any of my decisions. I also made sure my edibles jar was packed full to keep them mellow all weekend long if need be.

My girls pulled up only about an hour late, which I considered right on time for them. I met them on the front porch for hugs and pictures to kick off our long weekend. Their arms were overflowing with flowers from Pike's Market, which explained their tardiness. They all looked fabulous, as usual, and 'oohed' and 'aahed' over all the changes that we'd made since they'd seen the farm last. I had snacks laid out and a pitcher of sangria ready to go on the deck as we all found a cozy spot after they were unpacked and settled.

"Please tell me you have some eye candy lined up for us," Ash begged as we all laughed, and she poured herself another sangria. "Y'all laugh but I'm serious!"

"You sound like Lindsey! Erik and his Assholes will be here Saturday evening for the crab boil, there are some definite hotties this round," I suggested lewdly, adjusting my new cowboy hat that they brought me from Texas. *Maybe I AM a pimp!*

"Ooooo… you mean that sexy thang that was Jake's friend, what's his name again?" Ash asked.

"Erik," I replied without elaborating.

"Ooo yeah, Er–ik," Ash drug out each syllable of his name, "he's enough eye candy for all of us!"

"Oh yeah, I've met him here before," said Lindsey quietly. Her comment made me look at her a little more thoroughly. It wasn't like Linds to be so quiet about anything.

"He'll be here," I confirmed, making a mental note to get Lindsey alone for further questioning.

"Will he take us on a bike ride? I bet he can really *guide* us in a good direction," Ash added, thrusting her hips. *Do all women in their fifties sound as horny as my friends?*

The driveway alarm chimed letting me know someone had pulled up to the house. Shaking my head, I left the cackling queens to their jokes and went to see who it was. My mouth fell open when I saw the subject of our conversation standing in my driveway.

"Hey! What are you doing here?" I asked, walking up as Erik grabbed his duffle bag out of the back seat.

"Hi, love," he said, closing his door. He stopped when he saw me and grinned. "Nice hat."

"Thanks," I said, tipping it to him. "If you're lucky, I might keep it on later," I drawled while wiggling my eyebrows. He swung his arm around my shoulder, looked around to make sure the coast was clear, and brought me in for a heated kiss. "I tried texting and calling but you never replied, so I called Larry, and he said you were with your mates." We walked up to the front porch with his arm still slung over my shoulder. I breathed him in, that same body wash I remember from his shower. *Yum!* "Sorry, I forgot they were going to be here. I should have called before I got on the ferry," he added, stopping before we got to the front door.

"It's fine and I *am* glad to see you," I smiled, "it'll just be tricky acting like I don't want to rip your clothes off in front of these jackals that I call friends," I laughed and kissed him quickly on his smirking lips. "You ready for show time?"

He regarded me for a moment before answering, "It might be fun to watch you squirm... I'm in and keep the hat on." *This didn't sound good... or did it?*

We walked out to the deck just in time. The sangria pitcher was running low, and I had been gone too long. The ladies were complaining and starting to get up to search for me. Luckily, Erik snagged the second pitcher from the fridge.

"Our hero!" sang Ash, as Erik filled everyone's glasses including an extra I grabbed for him.

"Erik, you remember my girls: Diane, Ash, and Lindsey. Y'all know Erik." He gave a cute, little bow that made us all giggle. I guess the wine was starting to kick in. I'm sure it didn't help that I hadn't had much to eat all day. I sat back down in my designated seat which only left Erik a seat on the sofa between Diane and me.

"We weren't expecting you, why did you come early?" asked Diane, taking a particularly large gulp of her red drink. Luckily, I had another pitcher in the outside fridge.

"I don't usually make it a practice to come early," he said slyly, giving me a side-eyed glance. I couldn't stop my bark of laughter, but I think my girlfriends only had eyes for Erik and didn't get the innuendo, "But I missed Kelly so much, I couldn't wait another day to see her," he grinned, patting my leg next to his. I rolled my eyes as my traitorous friends giggled like teenagers.

"I love your accent, Erik. How long have you lived in the States?" fluttered Ash.

"Nearly ten years. My mum and family still live in England," he answered patiently. I lit the fireplace and divvied out blankets while they peppered him with questions. The sangria was going down smoothly, and we polished off the third pitcher sooner rather than later. Conversation drifted from Erik to our families back to Erik then our work, back to Erik... I shifted in my seat to get more comfortable, my body longed to touch him. *Fuck it.* I turned my body on the couch and put my legs across Erik's lap under the blanket. It was obvious that I had moved, but I was trying to make it seem as casual as possible. No one seemed to bat an eye... that is, except for Erik. He held his glass of the fruity wine above the blanket and discreetly moved his other hand to my leg underneath and squeezed. *Fucking Niagara Falls.*

"Erik, are you married or have a girlfriend?" asked Diane, my eyes cut over in her direction, but it seemed an innocent question.

"I'm divorced, no girlfriend," he replied, squeezing my leg again higher on my thigh. I looked around quickly, but no one seemed wise to his hand placement.

"What kind of eye candy are you going to have for us on Saturday?" I asked in a slightly gruff voice, changing the subject to something I knew would get their attention.

"Eye candy?" Eric murmured. "Aren't you taking this pimp thing a bit too far?"

I laughed out loud. "It was their question not mine!" My girls nodded in agreement.

"We're married, not blind!" yelled Ash. *Exactly.*

Erik started ticking the names from his mental list of the eight guys that would be there on Saturday for the crab boil. I had met them all, so I was giving feedback on their... attributes with comical commentary. We laughed well into the night until the sangria was gone and our eyes drooped with sleep.

"Where are you sleeping, Erik?" Diane asked as we cleaned up the kitchen. I felt like a runner that stumbled at the finish line. *Shit.*

"I'm hoping to snuggle up with Kelly... but if not, the couch downstairs in the basement," he taunted.

"You go, Kelly!" Ash called as she headed upstairs. "Goodnight everyone!" Lindsey and Diane followed right behind.

I smiled at Erik as he pulled me close, once we heard the doors close upstairs. "That was almost fun," he smirked, kissing me firmly on the mouth, "but I've wanted to do that all night." I smiled and kissed him back, deepening it, and gliding my hands up underneath his shirt.

"I bet you thought you were being so sneaky with those flirty little comments," I teased, nipping his earlobe and pulling it lightly.

"Honesty is the best policy," he murmured as he reached up my shirt and dipped his hand into the cup of my bra, grazing my nipple with his thumb. I moaned, pushing into him more. I slid my hands down and began to unfasten his pants.

"Thank you for keeping our secret." I licked his neck as I pulled down his zipper. "I guess I should repay you somehow." I reached in his pants and cupped Erik's throbbing member, eliciting a moan from its owner. "Let's go see what we can do with that," I whispered, as I bit down at the base of his neck. *Whoops, that might leave a mark.*

I didn't let go of Erik's cock as I guided him to my bedroom and to the foot of the bed, letting go only to slide his pants and briefs down his legs, allowing his beautiful penis to spring free. I lifted his shirt over his head, so that he was standing magnificently naked in front of me, waiting for my next move. I trailed my fingertips over all the indentions in his torso that he had chiseled with his physical abilities. I leaned in and licked my way down his abdomen, my cowboy hat falling to the floor forgotten, until I reached his protruding center. Lowering myself onto my knees, I looked up and met his gaze as I licked the tip of his manhood. He hissed and reached down pulling my shirt over my head. My boobs were pulled out of their cups from Erik's massaging in the kitchen, so I felt like a pinup girl with my bra pushing them higher. Erik's eyes were glazed with desire as he sat down on the bed and grasped my pale globes with both hands. He rolled my nipples between his fingers and groaned, then pushed his cock against my breasts as his eyes rolled back in his head.

I reached and cupped his jewels in my hand as I slid his rock, hard dick between my boobs. Erik gasped, pushing my breasts together as he thrust between them again. I licked the tip of his shaft when he pulled back and thrust up again, moaning my name. Erik continued thrusting as I sucked and licked his tip until he groaned and laid back on the bed pulling me on top of him.

"I need to be inside you," he gasped, breathless from his titty-fucking exertion, looking delicious laid out below me. Inspiration struck as I bounded off the bed.

"Where are you going?" he moaned, stroking his dick as he watched me. Hypnotized by his actions, I stood and watched as he increased his rhythm, his eyes unwavering from mine. I unfastened my jeans and pushed them over my hips, stepping out of them and pushing them away clumsily. *Real graceful, Kelly.* I stood there in only my bra that was still pushing my breasts up in that wanton fashion that Erik seemed to enjoy. I found the reason for my dismount lying on the floor. I reached down, scooping up my new cowboy hat and placed it on top of my head with a smirk.

"Howdy, cowboy," I drawled, swaggering closer to the bed. "I was hopin' you could give me a ride, darlin'," I teased, climbing onto the bed and crawling up his body. His hand was still holding his dick but not moving, his eyes as wide as they could be. I stopped when I straddled his waist and ground my mound against his hard staff moaning with the friction. A growl rumbled from his chest as he adjusted and plunged himself all the way to my center, forcing my hands to his chest to balance. He bucked again and I was ready this time, meeting his hips with my own as we found our rhythm.

"Fuck me," he groaned, as I rode his huge dick feeling my climax already starting to build. He sat up pulling me against him as he grabbed my shoulders to pull me down harder. I grabbed my new hat and put it on his head. *Goddamn, I love a cowboy.* I had never felt him so deep before, so connected. "I'm going to come," he whispered frantically, sliding his hand down and finding my clit with his thumb between us. "Come for me," he groaned, pressing it harder and rubbing as we still thrust together.

"Here I come, here I come..." I chanted as my orgasm enveloped my body. Erik shuttered against me as he came, thrusting against me slowly a few more times.

"Keep the hat," Erik said once our breathing became more regular, chuckling.

"I think I will," I agreed.

Elyse Rundell

Chapter 23

The sky was overcast the next morning as Erik headed off to the trail with his merry band of Assholes. Our farm is so close to the Olympic National Trail that Erik usually only needed transport one-way. My head was pounding from the wine, so I found the Advil in the cabinet and made sure to leave it on the kitchen counter. My friends and I had plans to get up early and start our day, but it seemed that the night's festivities were affecting us all. *Damn sangria.* I helped Larry with the morning chores after breakfast was laid out for our guests staying in our cabins.

"Thanks for the help, Kelly, but I got it from here," Larry said, grabbing my empty feed bucket from my hand. "Looks like you could use some more rest."

"Thanks, Larry. We're going to Port Townsend for brunch and shopping. You good for the crab boil tonight? Do you need anything from town?"

"We're good. As soon as Erik and his Assholes are ready, we'll throw them in the pot and eat!" Larry laughed, rubbing his belly. I loved that even Larry used the Asshole nickname.

"Throw who in the pot? The Assholes or the crabs?" I asked, smiling.

"Hell, both!" Larry laughed.

I freshened up and waited for the girls to come down for our day in Port Townsend, a fun, artsy seaside town that was nearby. It hadn't escaped my attention how quiet and 'un-Lindsey-like' Lindsey was last night. Hopefully I would find some time today to talk to her alone and find out what was going on. We stopped at a local bakery for coffee and danish to soak up our wine from last night before we walked down Water Street, looking at the array of eclectic shops that lined the waterfront street. We ended our outing at one of the local wineries just outside of town.

"Kelly, tell us more about Erik. He sure is one tall drink of water," Ash cooed while she sipped her sparkling white wine. I rolled my eyes. I had hoped I was in the clear of this topic of conversation.

"What do you want to know?" I asked, trying my best to sound casual.

"He sure does flirt with you," Diane said suspiciously. I nodded in response.

"Right? He's always been like that. So silly," I waved my hand hoping to change the subject.

"Does he always stay in the house with you?" she inquired further.

"Yep, for years now," I shrugged nonchalantly and took a rather large gulp of my wine. The cool, bubbly liquid felt good to my suddenly parched throat.

"Does he have any kids?" asked Ash.

"Nope. He said he's never wanted any," I grabbed my water bottle from my bag and took a few large swallows from it. *Damn this dry throat.*

Lindsey looked at me from across the table and gave me a rather sly smile. "I think you like him."

I met her sly smile with one of my own, since I was happy she had finally joined our conversation, "What's not to like?"

"Would you sleep with him if he made a move?" she countered, taking me by surprise.

"Do you think I should?" I made it a point to ask a question and not answer hers directly, though I was interested in what their responses would be.

"No!" yelped Diane as both Ash and Lindsey shouted "Yes!" *Shocker.* I laughed and took a long sip of my wine, hoping someone would change the subject.

"Could he be gay?" asked Diane.

I nearly choked on my sip. "I don't believe so, but maybe you should ask him," I laughed.

Diane changed the subject and off we went on another tangent. I noticed that Lindsey never did mention anything about her and Rick. Before long, we headed back to the farm to get ready for the crab boil. Picnic tables lined with newspaper, fresh steamed crabs straight out of the pot, friends and fellowship as everyone eats, drinks and has a helluva time. It was my idea of a great kind of party. I checked on Larry, who had already finished my chores. ("I can handle things while your friends are here.") *Have I mentioned I love him?*

Our neighbor, Daryl, was nice enough to drive the transport van to pick up Erik and the Assholes, especially with a couple of crab dinners and beer as payment. The girls and I got busy getting our party space set up. It was amazing what a few extra sets of hands can get accomplished. We had plenty of time to freshen up for the night, so we made a plan to meet at the boil.

Donning my new favorite cowboy hat, I headed out to see if I could lend Larry a hand, but he and Rosalie had everything under control. The sides were ready, the crab pot was boiling, and the beer was cold, we were just missing half of our guests. An hour late, the transport van pulled up the driveway and Erik and his Assholes unloaded.

"Hel–lo cowgirl… Sorry we're late," Erik smiled suggestively. Giving me a wink, he leaned in and whispered, "Daryl talks faster than he drives."

"I should have seen that coming," I laughed, "but beggars can't be choosers. I'm just glad for the help." Traffic couldn't be helped sometimes on the Peninsula, so a laid-back attitude came in handy.

It was decided we'd go ahead and eat, since we'd been waiting long enough. Larry threw the crabs in the pot and a feast was had by all.

"I swear, Larry. I'd keep you around just for your crab skills alone," I cried as I dumped what was left of my crab carcass into the compost bin. The Assholes were cleaning up from their ride and dinner back in their cabins, and the rest of us were sitting around the bonfire chatting with full beers and even fuller bellies.

"Erik, why didn't you get changed?" Ash asked as she took a chair in the growing circle around the fire.

"I was hoping Kelly could give me a bath later," he taunted. I rolled my eyes at him and pulled my hat down lower as everyone laughed at his obvious joke. Then, I gave him a side-glance with a wink when he met my eye. *Yes, please.*

The Assholes started trickling back and our bonfire circle grew larger and larger. Lindsey seemed more upbeat this evening, and even told a story from our college days that made Larry almost pee his pants. The night wore on with drinking and talking and laughing. I noticed that conversation between Lindsey and a handsome, blonde Asshole had been going on for a while. I knew things had been rough with her husband, Rick, but she wasn't the type that would step out on him. *No judgment zone, Kelly. She can make her own decisions.*

"Let's turn on some music. I wanna dance!" yelled Rosalie, grabbing Larry's hand and jumping up and down. He nearly fell out of his chair as his whole body shook from her over-the-top movements.

"God damn, woman's going to kill me," Larry mumbled to Erik as he attempted to fumble out of his seat but gave up and sat back down. I turned on the music from my phone to our outdoor speakers, and a catchy pop tune filled the air. Rosalie attempted to twerk in front of Larry, backing up and nearly sitting in his lap.

"Ah mate, but it'll have been a hell of a ride," Erik laughed as Larry's face turned beet red when the twerking turned into a full-on lap dance. Deciding to save what was left of Larry's dignity, I steered Rosalie toward an open space for a makeshift dance floor. I beckoned my friends to join us as we danced along to the upbeat music. After a few songs, it was all us girls and the blonde Asshole dancing, having a fantastic time. The music changed abruptly and a slow, country classic started drifting through the night air. I kicked myself for downloading the app to Larry's phone as I saw his smug grin. He walked over and twirled Rosalie until she was settled up against him, swaying in his beefy arms. *Romantic bastard.*

"May I have this dance?" murmured a delectable voice in my ear.

"Do you remember how?" I asked, turning around, I placed my hand on Erik's shoulder. He placed one hand on my waist and clasped my other hand.

"I had a good teacher," Erik replied huskily, pulling me closer. The musky scent of his sweaty body filled my nostrils, and I felt heat begin to build between my legs. *Damn, even his smelly body turns me on.* We two-stepped around the small dance floor trying to avoid the other dancers. We weren't ready for any competition, but we were holding our own.

"Careful… everyone is going to think we're up to something," I murmured as I saw Rosalie give us a side-eye glance when we danced around her and Larry.

"They'll just think *I'm* up to no good," he growled low in my ear.

"What else is new?" I snorted, making Erik laugh and shake his head.

"Ex-act-ly," he whispered. "We act like this out in the open and they won't expect we're sneaking around," he chuckled. "Lindsey's mood seems lifted tonight," Erik said softly, slowing our steps and swaying to the slower love song that had started.

"I thought the same thing. Think it has anything to do with a certain blonde Asshole that hasn't left her side?" I asked, glancing over at the two in question dancing off to the side of the dance floor away from the others.

"I'm sure of it," he replied, slowly turning us so my back was to them.

"She's been having problems with Rick," I said, trying to turn Erik again for a better view of the people in question. "Should I say something to her or just let her make her own bad decisions?" I asked earnestly. He answered with a tender smile.

"I think you know what my answer is." We kept swaying, looking into each other's eyes. The glow of the party lights hanging from above made his brown eyes seem darker.

"Fine, I'll leave her be. Rick has always been a jerk anyway," I concluded. The song changed (thanks to Rosalie snagging Larry's phone) and a fast tempo club beat began. I shimmied against Erik as he stood immobile, unsure yet on whether he should stay for the torture of dancing with us or go find a seat amongst the safety of the men. I danced around to his back, wrapped my arms around his waist and drug my hands down his torso making the decision for him. He was still wearing his tight spandex biking outfit, so I could feel every muscled indentation beneath the sheer fabric. Erik stopped my hands from moving any lower as he gripped my hand and spun me around and around until I landed in his arms with my back to his front.

"*Much* better," he murmured in my ear as we swayed to the music. "Now let's go back to this 'you giving me a bath' idea. Bloody brilliant," he groaned, as he nuzzled my neck. I laughed and pushed away from him to dance with my friends.

"You sure have been dancing it up with Er–ik," crowed Ash as I joined the ladies in their dance circle.

"He's a good dancer. You should ask him yourself," I laughed as I bumped her hip with mine. We danced to a few more songs before we all agreed it was time to clean up.

Diane and Ash were the first to call it a night. They weren't normally night owls, so the last few late nights made them need some sleep to recharge. Most of the Assholes and Daryl and June weren't far behind them and having made sure everything was good for the night, Larry and Rosalie headed off to their cabin. Erik and I were left with Lindsey and her blonde Asshole, and they were walking our way.

"Can we talk for just a minute… alone?" she asked quietly.

"Of course," I said, glancing at Erik, who was already engaged in conversation with Lindsey's blonde friend. She followed me into the garden, where we followed the low-lit path that ambled its way through the overflowing raised beds, providing a feeling of privacy.

"Rick's moved out, we're getting a divorce," Lindsey blurted. My eyes widened in shock. I knew they were having problems, but I didn't realize just how much it had escalated.

"Oh, Linds! Are you okay?"

"I'm getting there. You know our marriage has been dying for a while, but him sleeping with one of the sales girls put the nail in the coffin," she said and shrugged, "I guess I jinxed myself when I said I hoped he would cheat." Lindsey took a sip of her drink and nodded toward the blonde Asshole, "Hottie McHotterson over there is giving me a much needed ego boost tonight."

"I've noticed," I smiled, pulling her in for a hug. "I'm guessing this is why you've been so distracted this weekend?" I asked.

"Yeah, sorry. I've just had so much on my mind," she sighed and took another gulp of her drink nervously.

"Don't worry about it," I smiled. "Now... *Why* are we over here by ourselves when there are two hot men over there that want to have their way with us?"

Lindsey gasped; her mouth flew open in shock. "You and Erik?" she finally managed. I nodded.

"For a couple of months now," I smiled. "Just fun, nothing serious...We'll talk more tomorrow, and I'll tell you everything."

"Sounds like we have stories to swap. I love you, Kel," she sighed as I brought her in for another hug.

"I love you too, Linds."

We walked back over to our awaiting suitors, and Lindsey and Blondie said their goodnights. Erik raised an eyebrow at me as we watched them walk away. I gave him my sweetest smile as I grabbed my phone. Soon, another slow, country ballad wafted across the speakers. The party lights glowed high above casting a romantic glow across the makeshift dance floor.

"One more dance before we call it a night?" I asked.

"Absolutely, my love," he replied. Meeting me on the dance floor, he snatched my hat off and placed it on his head and gathered me in his arms. We swayed to the music, hugging one another tight, not moving our feet.

"Lindsey and her husband are getting divorced," I said into Erik's chest. "She may just be using your friend for sex," I teased.

"I think he's okay with that," Erik kissed the top of my head. "It might not be a love for the ages, but I'm sure they will have a marvelous time," he added. We stayed that way until the end of the song, not saying a word, just swaying.

"Speaking of a marvelous time," I invited with a mischievous grin, taking back my cowboy hat. "Would you settle for a shower instead of a bath?"

"Absolutely, my love," he replied again. I turned the music off and took his hand, leading him toward the house. I stopped abruptly at the door causing his body to collide with mine. I bent over gently and rubbed my ass up against his front, eliciting a deep, satisfying groan from behind me as he grabbed my hips. I turned my head slightly, peering back at him over my shoulder.

"Whoops, sorry about that...," I purred and bit my lip as I opened the front door. I rubbed up again before taking a step inside when Erik crushed me to his front clutching my breast with one hand as his other reached between my legs. I could feel his erection through his tight shorts as we moved together.

"My little vixen," he moaned, gripping the denim between my legs harder. "I'd fuck you right here if I weren't so dirty," his voice was raspy with desire as he bit my neck. I could have melted on the spot, but the anticipation of having Erik naked in my shower was enough to spur me forward.

"Almost there...," I sighed as I pushed back against him roughly, making him gasp and loosen his arms. I spun around grabbing Erik's hand and pulled him forward. I'd always had a fantasy of peeling him out of one of these tight outfits, and it was about to come true. We were a tangled knot of arms, hands and feet as we attempted to remove our shoes once we made it to my room, all the while our mouths never left one another. My back hit the wall as Erik unfastened my jeans and plunged his hand inside finding my wet center. "Fuck!" I gasped as he shook his fingers against my throbbing clit. I couldn't resist. I pushed my pelvis against his hand and rode the pleasure of my climax until I shuttered, my body sagging against him.

Erik pulled his hand from my pants. I could see two of his fingers were wet from my orgasm as he slid them into his mouth and sucked, sliding his tongue between them both.

"So good," he murmured and reached down to remove his shorts.

"Wait," I scolded, "I want to do that." I grabbed Erik's hands and pulled him to the bathroom. Turning on the water for the shower, I wiggled the rest of the way out of my jeans and let them fall to the floor. Walking up to Erik, I slid my eyes down taking in his well-muscled legs clad with the black spandex that hugged every curve. I reached out and slid my hands under his shirt pushing it slowly up his body until he helped pull it over his head. I ran my tongue down his smooth torso, tasting his salty skin. Dipping my fingers into the waistband of his tight shorts, I peeled them down, allowing his massive erection to spring out and then on down to reveal his smooth, muscled legs.

"I've been wanting to do that for a while," I whispered, biting my lip. I quickly took off my bra and panties and stepped into the warm water of the shower. Erik stood in silence looking surprised. "Are you coming?" I asked, looking over my shoulder. He snapped out of his reverie and grinned.

"Not yet, love," he teased as he stepped behind me into the warm water. He snaked his arms around my body and cupped my breasts then slid his fingers over my wet skin. "How long is a while?" he murmured in my ear as he continued his exploration.

"What do you mean?" I asked, distracted by his wicked hands.

"You said you've 'been wanting to do that for a while', how long is a while?" Erik asked as he kissed my neck.

"I don't know," I shrugged, squirming my hips against his front. *He doesn't need to know how long I've fantasized about him.* Grabbing the body wash, I soaped up my hands and turned around. "Let's get you cleaned up," I smiled. I soaped nearly every inch of Erik's beautiful body. His wandering hands had my body just as soapy... and just as worked up. I saved the best for last, grasping Erik's thick cock in my soapy hands. I stroked it to the tip and back down again making sure it was squeaky clean. I reached lower and cradled his balls as I lightly squeezed and massaged them, biting his lower neck. Feeling emboldened, I stroked his cock again as I reached around and slid a soapy hand down his taut ass, massaging it as I stroked his cock. I reached further and slid a finger down his ass crack leaving a soapy trail as I went. I stroked faster as I slid the tip of my finger into his asshole as a hiss escaped Erik's clenched teeth. I eased it in just a bit further and he moaned.

"Kel–ly... I need you." I turned around and bent over, grasping the edge of the shower ledge as Erik let the warm water rinse away the soap. He grabbed my shoulder and a fistful of my hair as he slid his hard dick into my pussy. "Fuuuck, you're so tight," he groaned.

"Aw, yes," I gasped as I pushed against him, bringing him deeper. He thrust in and out of me as I met him thrust for thrust. Erik reached down and swatted my ass once then again harder as he poured himself into me calling my name with me following closely behind. We stayed that way, Erik leaning over against my back, as we let the warm water cascade around us. He stood up and eased out of me causing me to gasp from the sensation.

"That was fun," he sighed, kissing my neck when I stood up. He massaged my shoulders as I stretched under the water... my muscles now loose from my orgasm. "Are you going to tuck me into bed now?" he taunted. I turned around to fire a comeback at his silly joke, when he clasped his hands to my face and kissed me tenderly on the lips over and over.

"I don't remember what I was going to say," I murmured against his lips.

"That was my goal," he grinned against my mouth. Sleep came quickly to us both as soon as our heads hit the pillow.

Chapter 24

Dawn broke a little too early the morning after the crab boil. My body felt sinfully sore after our shower the previous night… and a quick fuck in the wee hours of the morning. I was tired, but unfortunately, the quiches for my guests weren't going to make themselves. I looked over at the sexy man lying next to me when inspiration struck.

"Good morning," I murmured as I kissed Erik's neck.

"Good god woman, you are insatiable," he moaned, keeping his eyes closed. "But give me one minute and I'll rally," he grinned his sexiest, lazy grin. *God he's gorgeous.*

"I have to get up and make breakfast," I said in my poutiest voice as I continued my path down his neck. "If only I had a strong, smart, handsome man to come be my sous chef. I'm sure I'd get done *way* faster."

Erik groaned, "If only there was a task, or a *job* per se, that you could do to entice this strong, *virile* man to be your sous chef." He pulled the sheet down to show "Little Erik" standing at attention.

I looked up at him and grinned, "You better chop fast."

"Yes, chef."

We had the quiches in the oven in record time, thanks to my sous chef's quick knife work. He even helped prepare the fruit trays while I made coffee.

"Those are some sweet skills you've got there," I teased as he finished cutting up the melon.

"I could say the same to you, vixen. Feel free to entice me anytime," he replied and kissed me firmly. I heard footsteps coming down the stairs, so I took a step away from what I'd rather have for breakfast.

"God! Y'all are both up already," complained Diane as she and Ash came down the stairs.

"Good morning to y'all too, Mary Sunshine," I smiled and placed two mugs of coffee on the kitchen island. "Is Lindsey up yet?"

"Not yet. I knocked on her door, and she said she was sleeping in. How late did y'all stay out?" asked Ash as she doctored her coffee. Luckily, she was too distracted to see the look I gave Erik.

"You know, I have no idea," I fibbed. I didn't think Diane and Ash knew about Lindsey's split, and I wasn't going to be the one to tell them. "It *was* late though." The timer on the oven beeped signaling my quiches were done. *Perfect timing!*

"Y'all go on outside to the table on the deck, and we'll bring out the food," I said to Diane and Ash. "Drinks of all sorts are set up outside and I have the heaters on so it's cozy."

"I better get another blow job out of this," Erik groaned in my ear as my friends headed outside.

"I'm sure that can be arranged," I smiled. "I was going to make Linds and her friend a tray of food and get you to run it up. Do you mind?" I pleaded, batting my eyelashes innocently. "I promise I'll make it up to you later," I whispered as I slid my hand down his chest.

Erik shook his head and grinned. "You really are a vixen. Hurry and I'll take it up," he resigned. I kissed him quickly on his firm lips and jumped into action. Quick tray for Linds and Blondie and he was on his way upstairs. Nothing fancy but it got the job done. I grabbed a couple of platters and dished up enough quiche to take for us outside and joined my friends at the table.

"Breakfast is served," I announced, placing the platters of quiche and fruit on the table. Diane and Ash had already helped themselves to mimosas, while they waited.

"What did we miss last night?" asked Ash as she filled her plate. Erik walked out and gave me a wink as he sat next to me at the table. I had one last place set for Lindsey, but I wasn't sure if the blonde, boy toy would join us. *Doubt it.*

"Not a whole lot, just more dancing," I replied, taking a bite of the quiche so I didn't have to elaborate.

"Linds was certainly having a good time with that blonde fella," said Diane, lowering her voice.

"We were all having fun," I retorted.

"Well, it didn't look good is all. She was giving people the wrong impression," Diane insisted.

"I'm sure it was innocent," replied Ash. "She wouldn't do anything to hurt Rick like that." I remained quiet and took a sip of my coffee. Ash always tried to see the good in everyone.

"She might do something if Rick was a dick," said Erik casually, then took a sip of his coffee. I slid Erik a grin. I wanted to plant a huge kiss on his smug, sexy face, but that would only add fuel to Diane's fire.

"And Rick *is* a dick, it doesn't *just* rhyme," I giggled then stopped when I saw the look Diane sent my way. "I'm sure Linds will fill us in on all the juicy details when she comes down," I conceded, at least I hoped she would.

"So, Erik, I'm surprised you're still here. When do you head back to Seattle?" Diane asked in her usual highbrow way.

"I'm going back tomorrow," Erik smiled then added, "I have a last-minute kayaking tour to give this afternoon."

"Single and no children," Diane pressed, "Kelly said you don't want children of your own. Why not? I don't understand people like you."

My eyes widened at Diane's question and statement. *What the hell?* I glanced around the table, and it seemed that Ash and Erik were both just as dumbstruck. Diane was the only one that seemed unfazed by the rudeness of what she just said, taking another dainty bite of quiche as she waited for Erik's response.

"Yeah, we're an odd lot. Never wanted any kids and never will... my siblings have had enough for us all," he said calmly and took another sip of his coffee while the table was silent. "I should go for a run before it gets any later. Kelly?" I looked up as Erik met my gaze. "Will you walk me inside?"

"Sure," I said, grabbing another quick sip of my coffee. *I might need to switch to something stronger.* I followed Erik inside as he walked past the living room straight to my bedroom and closed the door after me. "I'm sorry about, Di–," I was cut off by Erik's mouth crashing against mine pushing me back until he laid me down on the bed.

"I'm not a fan of your mate," he murmured as he kissed his way down my body. My clothes were a barrier between us, but it didn't slow down the desire that was starting to build. *What the hell?*

"She can be a bit much sometimes," I whimpered as he bit at the apex of my thighs through my yoga pants then continued his tortuous path down my legs. *What was he doing?*

Erik stood up over me and knocked my sandal to the floor as he grabbed my foot and lifted my leg. He used both hands to quickly massage my foot, in the arch, then the pad of my foot, he trailed a finger along my sole, tickling me. I tried to pull my foot away, but he laughed and repeated the torture. I could see the desire in his eyes as I tried to pull away again.

"Not so fast, vixen," he murmured as he started massaging my foot again. "I'm collecting my payment for being your errand boy this morning."

"Erik, I don't have time–," I began.

"Oh, I know. This won't take long," he murmured as he bent his head and bit my big toe. My hips bucked up as if a jolt of electricity shot through my foot to my groin. He captured my toe in his mouth and sucked as he massaged my foot. *Fucking Niagara Falls.* Erik then abruptly dropped my foot back on the bed.

"Hey!" I yelped.

"My payment," he taunted, "is knowing that you're sitting out there, hot and bothered, listening to your friends jabber on while your panties are wet." He reached down and touched me *there* with his thumb and groaned, "Fucking wet," then pulled it away.

I groaned, pushing my hips toward him involuntarily. Hot and bothered was right. I lifted my foot that his tongue lashed and nudged the enlarged bulge in the front of his shorts gently causing a hiss to escape his sexy mouth. I guess I wasn't the only one hot and bothered.

My phone, buzzing with an incoming message, distracted us from our game. It was Lindsey, asking for help on getting her friend out of the house unseen.

"I'll make sure he gets out when I leave. You make sure your friends stay drinking on the deck," Erik commanded, while I stood up and adjusted myself.

"Aye, aye captain," I purred in Erik's ear as I cupped his still hardened bulge and squeezed before walking out of the bedroom to distract my friends.

"Vixen!" he howled. *I might pay for that later... hopefully.*

"What was that?" Ash asked as I joined them back at the table. I poured myself a mimosa and added extra champagne. *Fuck it.*

"Erik stubbed his toe. He'll be fine," I waved it off as I sipped my cocktail. "He's going for a run and will be back later."

"A run? I don't run unless I'm being chased," giggled Ash as she topped off her mimosa.

"Right there with you. He jokes it's to maintain his girlish figure," I laughed.

"I'll be the first to say," Diane announced holding up her champagne flute, "there is nothing *girlish* about his figure."

"Cheers to *that!*" I agreed clinking her glass with mine, forgiving her for her unfiltered mouth.

"What are we cheers-ing to?" asked Lindsey as she joined us at the table.

"Well, looky what the cat drug in," cooed Ash. "Long night?"

"You could say that," nodded Lindsey cryptically. "Could someone pour me a drink? I need to catch y'all up on a few things."

Lindsey told us nearly everything. From her unhappiness with Rick in their marriage, to his affair and her indifference, and finally to the separation and upcoming divorce. She failed to mention Blonde Asshole to Diane and Ash, but I was one to talk since they didn't know about Erik either.

"I always thought Rick was an asshole!" swore Diane. *Yeah right.* Diane had always swooned over Rick whenever he was around.

"I'm sorry to hear that you had to go through all that, Linds," comforted Ash. "We'll have to all go do something together once your divorce is final," her eyes lit up.

Lindsey smiled, "Yeah, we'll definitely do that."

"Kelly," Erik called from inside the house. I had heard him get back from his run while Lindsey was telling her tale, so I assumed he got Blondie out with no problems... except the one in his pants. "I'm taking the Arseholes kayaking. Larry's picking us up later."

"Have fun!" I called back.

"Is he taking the same guys from last night?" asked Ash.

"Yep", "Yeah" both Lindsey and I responded. I looked up and met Lindsey's eye and they crinkled into a smile, neither Ash nor Diane noticed. "They'll be back later this afternoon," I continued. "I should have asked if y'all wanted to go kayaking. I'm sure they could have made room." We looked at each other with straight faces, then all busted out laughing at once.

"I *would* like to take a walk around the farm," said Ash looking around.

"Me too. We'll be back, ladies," assumed Diane in her Diane way. They got up and walked down the steps of the deck toward the creek.

"Spill it, quick!" I hissed to Lindsey.

She rushed it out, "It was… fun. A little awkward here and there, but a really good time. He's going to see if he can ride back with Erik tomorrow and stay another night."

"Wow! Are you going to tell Ash and Diane?"

"I haven't decided," she admitted.

"Me either," I confessed. "Maybe we should just tell them and endure Diane's judgment together."

"That sounds like an awful idea," Lindsey laughed. We agreed not to say a word.

Elyse Rundell

Chapter 25

Grilled chicken and cold pasta salad awaited Erik and his Assholes when they returned from their kayaking adventure. It had been an unusually warm day on the Peninsula, so the food fit nicely. Lindsey had suggested we bring the spread to the weary kayakers for a change of scenery. It took a little convincing, but she managed to talk Diane and Ash into joining the fun. The Assholes were unloading at their cabin when we walked up with my picnic wagon filled to the brim with food, drinks and all the accruement needed for a nice spread, and we quickly began setting up one of the outdoor tables.

"How are your panties?" a familiar English accent murmured softly behind my ear. Goosebumps immediately sprang up on my arm and my nipples hardened. *Fucker.* I narrowed my eyes at Erik but could not think of a witty enough reply. "Thank you for the walk-up service," he said softly when I didn't respond. "We weren't expecting anything."

"I was feeling *extra* nice today," I smirked with a sly wink. "I reserved this cabin for y'all tonight too since it was empty… in case anyone wanted to stay another night," Erik returned my smirk with a sexy one of his own as he took another big bite of chicken.

"Delicious," he murmured as his eyes burned into mine. He turned and took a seat at the picnic table while the Assholes entertained us with stories of their adventures. We enjoyed the atmosphere and cooler breeze as the sun moved lower in the sky.

When everyone was finished, I packed up my wagon to cart the leftovers home and began the walk up the hill. Erik's Assholes were packing up and one truckload had already left, when Erik approached and took the handle out of my hand. "I'll take this up for you," he said, then added in a hushed voice, "Lindsey has been invited to stay in the cabin tonight with her new friend. Do you mind?"

"Not at all," I whispered back. "Bring him up to the big house for drinks. I can manage the wagon," I smiled.

"I know exactly what you can manage, vixen," he smirked. "We'll be up in a jif. I still need to hear about your panties," he whispered, leaning closer. He handed the wagon handle back to me with his stupid, sexy smirk and jogged back to the others still at the cabin.

I shook my head as I turned and followed the girls back up to the big house. I emptied the wagon and stowed everything away while my friends got comfortable on the deck. I packed my vaporizer and took a seat with them outside.

"Do you really have to do that?" asked Diane, turning her nose up at me as she took another large gulp of wine.

"My house, my rules... remember?" I smiled. Diane had never been a fan of my love for cannabis. I had been tempted to bust out one of my big water bongs just to mess with her but thought better of it. I wanted to give my liver a break from alcohol for the night.

"Kelly, did you ever end up going out with the local guy... I don't remember his name," Lindsey asked, already refilling her wine glass. *Liquid courage for later?*

"Ray. Yeah, we went out a few times," I inhaled deeply, hoping someone would change the subject.

"*And?*" asked Ash. I looked up and all three were waiting for me to continue, their eyes wide with anticipation. *Too much to hope that they would let that one go.*

"He's nice... we had some pleasant conversations," I took a sip of my water. "He just doesn't do it for me."

"What do you mean?" asked Diane, rolling her eyes. *Fuck it.*

"He's boring in the bedroom, Diane," I stated bluntly. "Ray's a... no foreplay/no fun kinda guy... when I'm looking for a fuck me in the shower, toe-sucking, talk dirty to me kinda guy," I growled at the end and thrust my hips lewdly.

"You had sex with him!?" Lindsey practically yelled. *Whoops!* I forgot that I hadn't told them that part.

"Yes… a few months ago. Trust me, there's really not that much to tell." I rolled my eyes this time and took another drag from my vaporizer letting the mellowness wash over me.

"Are you still seeing him?" asked Ash, her eyes still wide with surprise.

"Just around town," I shook my head. "I told him when we first went out that I wasn't interested in anything exclusive."

"What do you mean nothing exclusive?" asked Diane tightly.

I took another drag from my vaporizer. One, to annoy Diane and two, to gather my thoughts. "I'm not looking to recreate my twenty-seven-year marriage. I'm starting over… slutting it up for a while," I smiled slyly.

"What if Mr. Toesucker comes along? Are you going to settle down with him or will you still be slutting it up?" asked Ash with a chuckle. I smiled to myself.

"If he comes along right now, then Mr. Toesucker will just have to wait," I chuckled.

"What am I waiting for?" came an irresistible, English voice from the side gate. Erik walked up with Blonde Asshole in tow.

"Kelly's looking for a toe sucker," Ash confided, laughing as I shot her a dirty look. Erik took the chair next to mine as Blondie took the seat that was conveniently vacant next to Lindsey.

"Looks like you found him, love," Erik murmured loud enough for the group to hear as he nabbed my vaporizer and took a long drag. Everyone chuckled at what they assumed was a joke, and Diane turned her attention

towards Mark or was it Matt? Blondie. She started
peppering him with questions, but I was too distracted by
Erik's proximity to pay attention. He handed me back my
vape and let our fingertips linger. I shifted my gaze up to
his as he laid his sexiest smirk on me. *Fucking Niagara
Falls.*

"You're *married?*" Lindsey's question caught the
attention of both Erik and I as we swung our heads around
to catch up with the conversation. She was directing it
towards her Blonde Asshole.

"I am but we're separated. The divorce isn't final
yet," he explained shyly.

"That sounds familiar," I suggested as I took
another long hit. They all cut their eyes over to me as I
shrugged my shoulders and exhaled.

"Everyone has a story to tell," Ash said finally, with
a big yawn, "But I'm too tired to hear any more. I'm
heading to bed." She got up off her seat on the couch and
folded her blanket.

"I'll head up with you. I'm exhausted," Diane
sighed. "We'll see y'all in the morning."

"I'll have breakfast ready... Good night," I called as
they both headed in the sliding door with a chorus of other
"good nights" from the others.

"Want to go for a walk?" Blondie asked Lindsey
right after the girls left with a pleading look on his face. I
nearly laughed out loud at his eagerness.

"Sure," Lindsey murmured and rolled her eyes.
They both stood up and walked out of the side gate where
Erik and he had come, presumably headed back to the
cabin.

"*Finally,* all alone," Erik murmured as he knelt on the floor between my knees and hugged me close.

"*Finally,*" I murmured as I ran my fingers through his hair and pulled his face to mine for a steamy kiss. Our tongues danced together exploring each other as I moaned against him.

"Tell me more about your panties," he groused as he nuzzled his way down my body. "Did they stay wet for me?"

"I had to change," I whimpered as he nuzzled between my legs. My hands were still fisted in his hair, so I pulled him closer to relieve the pressure that was building.

"Naughty girl…" he growled and bit at my crotch as he pulled me closer to the edge of the chair.

"What are you going to do about it?" I asked bravely, pushing his head toward my needy center. He chuckled as he sat back and grabbed my foot. I leaned back in my chair as he lifted my leg and drug it up his body.

"Where did we stop earlier?" he asked with a raised eyebrow. My heart raced as all the blood rushed to my groin. "Mr. Toesucker?"

I laughed. "You heard that?"

Erik had removed my sandal and was massaging my foot slowly. "Just enough," he murmured as he pulled my foot to his mouth. He bit my big toe like he had done that morning and pulled it into his mouth while he sucked it. I felt that same pulse straight to my groin. I nearly came right there. "Are your panties wet now, naughty girl?" he purred. I could only nod in response. I didn't trust my voice at the moment. He stood up and slid my foot down his body until it touched the hard bulge in his loose pants. He ground my foot against it as he gave me his sexy smirk. "Get your arse in that bedroom before I spank it," he demanded with a wicked glint in his eye.

"Promises, promises..." I sighed as I stood up and cupped his clad manhood. "A spanking might just be what I need to teach me a lesson," I taunted. Erik smiled and shook his head.

"Maybe next time... I need to fuck you *right* now," he groaned as he grabbed my hand and led me to my bedroom, where he did what he promised... a few times.

Elyse Rundell

Chapter 26

The house was quiet when I woke up the next morning. I left Erik asleep in my bed looking heavenly all wrapped in my sheets and decided to get some of my morning chores done. I left the coffee brewing and a tray of pastries and fruit for my girls in case they got up sooner rather than later, while I headed out to the barn to start our day.

I returned shortly since Larry had already completed almost everything. *I love that man.* I was in the mudroom removing my rainboots, when I heard a commotion from inside the house.

"Whoa! Sorry! I was looking for Kelly!" Ash shrieked. "Sorry! *So* sorry!" I heard a door slam. *Oh shit.*

I slowly walked out of the mudroom to see Diane sitting on the couch with her coffee mug suspended in mid-air and Ash wide-eyed standing in the kitchen. They both just stared at me without saying a word. Erik walked around the corner from my bedroom pulling on a tight, white T-shirt with his jogging pants riding low on his hips.

"Did I not tell y'all that Erik and I are fucking?" I asked, feigning innocence, shrugging my shoulders. "I was sure I mentioned it."

Erik glanced around the room, then walked over to the coffee bar casually, slapping my ass as he passed. "I was right, love, this *is* fun," he smirked and began pouring himself a mug from the warm pot.

"I think we would have remembered *that*, Kelly!" said Ash, still red-faced from whatever she saw in my bedroom. I followed Erik over and poured myself another cup wishing I had something stronger. We heard the front door open and voices speaking softly. *Lindsey*. Erik leaned against the kitchen counter and sipped his coffee, smiling smugly as he enjoyed the show.

"Shhh... we'll just get coffee then head back," Lindsey said softly to Blondie as they walked into the room then stopped short when she saw she had an audience. "Good morning," she said with uncertainty to the room of wide eyes that were staring at them.

"What the–?" Ash began.

"What in the hell is going on around here?" yelled Diane. Lindsey shrugged, not knowing how to answer the question. *Fuck this.*

"I've been sleeping with Erik, and Lindsey has had relations with this young buck all weekend," I motioned towards Lindsey and Blondie as I continued, "I think that catches everyone up." I took a sip of my coffee as I heard Erik give a little chuckle beside me.

"He's *twenty* years younger than you!" trilled Diane. *Here we go.*

"Eighteen," I replied as I heard Erik mumble the same. I glanced over and met his half smile with my own.

"How long has this been going on?" asked Ash.

"A couple of months," I answered.

"Erik said he didn't have a girlfriend," Diane speculated, "So then what are y'all?"

"Friends with benefits," I admitted, as Erik cleared his throat. I glanced over to see his eyebrow raised in question. "Or fuck buddies," I tried to say with a straight face. *Fuck it.*

"Does he see other women?" Ash volleyed.

"I have no idea." I placed my hand across Erik's chest since he looked like he was about to say something, "and I don't want to know."

"What does he see in you?" asked Diane. We all turned around and looked at her. She wasn't asking in an insulting way. It sounded like she truly wanted to know. *Why was I getting all the questions? Lindsey was the one still married.*

"Sex, Diane," I said slowly.

"He can have sex with anyone, Kelly, look at him," she stated bluntly. "What does he see in *you*?" Her eyes wide with wonder.

Erik spoke before I could say anything, "She makes me laugh," he smiled. "She's smart as a whip though I hate to admit it. She's gorgeous," he paused and looked at me.

"She brings joy to everyone she meets. That's what I see in her." He closed the gap between us and kissed me tenderly on the lips. "Plus, she's a good lay," he grinned and kissed me again soundly while the rest of the room was silent. "I'll see you ladies next time… We're leaving in twenty, mate," he directed at Blondie. Erik walked back to my bedroom while my friends remained wide-eyed and silent.

"Would someone please say something?" I asked. I was expecting a spectrum of reactions, but silence was not one of them.

They all spoke at once. "Holy shit!", "Are you kidding me?", "You look happy." The latter being Lindsey's response.

We decided that this conversation would be best with mimosas. Ash poured while Lindsey and I went and said a quick goodbye to Erik and Blondie. Erik was wiggling into his tight bike shorts when I walked in the bedroom. *Good timing, Kelly.* I stood mesmerized as he pulled them into place and adjusted his jewels for comfort. My eyes lingered lower to take in his sexy, muscular legs… one of the first things I noticed about him. The bike shorts hugged his thighs as his hands cupped his manhood and his hips swayed… *What the hell?* I looked up and Erik was brandishing his sexiest smirk as he watched me ogle him.

"I feel like a piece of meat," he teased, "I like it."

I smiled, "That was some awfully nice things you said out there."

He looked at me thoughtfully, "I meant it," he said and waited a few seconds, "you are a good lay," he grinned. I kissed him and told him goodbye, with the promise of objectifying him upon his return in a couple of weeks. He and the Blonde Asshole were leaving to find a quick trail on their way back to Seattle.

I joined my friends on the deck mentally preparing myself for the interrogation and hoping that mimosas would help. The first question was hurled my way before my ass hit the seat.

"How did it happen?"

"Stop real quick," I demanded. "Why am *I* the one in the hot seat when Lindsey slept with a younger man too?"

"It's not going to be serious, right Linds?" asked Diane.

"Nope," shrugged Lindsey.

"See? I can't believe you've been hiding this from us! So how did it happen?" Diane asked again.

I took a swig of my mimosa and launched into our story giving them the highlights. They didn't interrupt the entire time, which had to be a record. "It's been around two months now, and everything seems to be going great," I concluded. "We see each other every other weekend and talk occasionally in between. I'm happy."

"What do your kids think about him?" asked Lindsey.

"No one knows! Y'all better not tell a soul either." Even they nearly laughed at that request. "We're just sleeping together... That's it."

"That didn't sound like 'just sleeping together' from all those sweet things he said about you," Ash swooned. "Sounds like he likes you." Her comment made me smile.

"I like him, but I'm just enjoying him while it lasts. I'm sure once he gets over whatever obligation he feels toward Jake to take care of me, he'll be on to greener pastures," I sighed and sat back in my chair.

"What obligation to Jake?" asked Lindsey as all eyes turned toward me again.

"Erik told Jake he would look out for me after he passed, not that I need him to, but I hope he's not just sticking around because he's trying to keep his promise… you know?"

"So, you think Erik is screwing you because he feels sorry for you? Are you serious?" Linds laughed.

"No, it's not that. I just wonder if part of the reason he's attracted to me is because of the obligation he feels toward Jake." I took a deep breath and shook my head. No need in psycho-analyzing my feelings for Erik after only a couple of months. "Why are we still discussing this? Y'all are making me think too much about him, and he's only my distraction when he's here. Like I said," I smiled, taking a sip of my mimosa, "I'm just enjoying the fun while it lasts. Speaking of which…" I wiggled my eyebrows at Lindsey. "We need details!"

Lindsey smiled and told her tale of how things started with Blondie the other day.

"Are you going to see him again?" asked Ash, staring at Lindsey unblinking. Diane still hadn't uttered a word since Lindsey began.

"Who knows? I wouldn't mind. The sex was great, but his foreplay was a little weird," she admitted.

"Weird, how?" Diane asked, finally speaking up.

"Maybe he was into the whole, older woman thing, but… he spoke…" Lindsey covered her face with her hands with embarrassment. "*Baby talk!*" she groaned. I didn't think we could have been more shocked than we already were. *Baby talk?*

"Like what do you mean? Give us an example," I inquired. I tried picturing Erik murmuring dirty things to me in baby talk, and even that image didn't do it for me.

"Let me think… Okay, *God,* this is embarrassing," Lindsey started, then took a big swig from her champagne flute. "Okay… *'I've been a bad, bad boy',*" she said in a high-pitched voice that sounded more like Mickey Mouse than a baby. Guffaws of laughter bellowed from us all as we stomped our feet shaking the entire deck. Tears flowed from our cheeks as we each took turns saying *'I've been a bad, bad boy'* in our best cartoony voices.

"Y'all can't tell anyone," Lindsey demanded and looked at me, "especially not Erik." *What?*

"Why not? He won't say anything," I whined.

"Nope. Don't tell him," she replied. I rolled my eyes but nodded in agreement. I wasn't sure how close Erik and Blondie were, but I would begrudgingly accept Lindsey's request.

"Sounds like Erik really doesn't want kids," Diane admitted and told Lindsey of Erik's response to her question from yesterday.

"It was a huge reason his marriage ended," I added. "He has a ton of nieces and nephews in England that he seems somewhat close to. I guess that's good enough for him."

"Why have this open relationship? It seems like y'all are crazy about each other. I don't get it," Ash said in an exasperated tone.

"We're good with the way things are for now and there's no clock that is ticking in the background… why not have fun together and see where life takes us when we're apart?" I asked. My mind flashed to him sucking my toes, and I shook myself to clear my mind. "I'm just going with the flow and digging the vibes. Can we just leave it at that?"

"Dirty hippy," Lindsey laughed.

"Damn straight," I winked

"You're really not bothered about the age difference?" asked Diane, sounding skeptical.

"I'm not. I don't even think about it most of the time. He's an old soul and I'm a young soul, somehow it works," I smiled.

"I say do it, girl!" exclaimed Ash, "Now do we need to go shopping for you a bigger bag? I bet his diapers are *huge*!" *THIS is the reaction I expected.* I decided to add fuel to the fire.

"That's because of his *big* dick," I remarked casually.

We laughed ourselves silly, including Diane, before deciding we needed to venture out. Larry was happy to drive our tipsy rears around to the different wineries in the area. We had a ton of fun, and it was a great way to round out their trip, since they were headed home the next day. We ended the evening by dragging out old college yearbooks and looking up people from school on social media late into the night. They left the next morning with hugs and a few tears with promises of planning a divorce trip for Lindsey as soon as the papers were signed.

Chapter 27

Before I knew it, six months had passed, and early spring was upon us on the Olympic Peninsula. Preparation for the tourist season was gearing up all around town, and Larry and I had been busy making plans and freshening up the farm for the crazy season ahead. The cabins were now fully booked until the end of fall, thanks in large part to the publicity from the gala last year. The farm wasn't the only thing moving along well in my life. My "fuck buddy" relationship with Erik was better than I could have imagined. We'd seen each other every other weekend barring a couple of months during the holidays when we were both traveling, and no one was the wiser.

It was a cool, crisp Friday night. Erik and I were sitting on either ends of the couch on the deck passing my water bong back and forth, relaxed in our pajamas. Larry and Rosalie were sitting in adjacent chairs polishing off a second bottle of cider that I had been given by Skyler's brewery.

"I'm not much for cider, but this stuff is nice," cooed Rosalie, smacking her lips. "Though free booze is always the best booze."

"That's the truth," slurred Larry. He wasn't normally such a cheap drunk, but he had hit my water bong a few times as well.

"I like it too. Skyler, Sam's girlfriend, is bottling it at their place," I bragged. Sam was coming up that weekend to stay with her, since Skyler had flown down to Texas multiple times during the off-season. "We're serving it tomorrow night at the party too, so no more tonight," I grinned at the lushes who were both nearly done with their glasses.

"Is that your Chamber of Commerce party?" Erik asked with a smoldering look in his eye. Larry and Rosy had been here since he arrived, so we'd been unable to give each other a proper greeting.

"Yep, we're hosting their annual Spring Bash. It should wrap up around nine, so not too late," I smiled, though it took every bit of will power I had not to touch him. "Larry, you're picking Erik and the Assholes up tomorrow, right?"

"Sure am. Are you going to the party, Erik? Should be a real *fun* time," Larry said sarcastically as he rolled his eyes and pretended to hang himself. I flipped him off with both hands with a grin. The Chamber folks were fun, just not Larry's cup of tea.

"We'll just have to see, mate," he laughed, looking over at me with another panty-wetting smile. I returned his smile with a seductive wink then looked over and met Rosalie's sly smile. *Busted.*

"*Ray* will be at the party, right Kelly?" she asked innocently. My eyes narrowed at her suspiciously.

"I'm sure he will," I replied casually.

"Maybe I *can* make an appearance," Erik muttered, smiling over at me mischievously. He must not have noticed Rosalie eyeing us both like a cat that swallowed the canary.

"Take me home, Larry," Rosalie announced abruptly. Larry looked taken aback at her sudden request, but he complied and shrugged his shoulders.

"See you tomorrow, guys," he said and snagged another couple of beers from the cooler as they walked away. Erik smiled and scooted closer to me once we heard the gate close. He tucked a lock of hair back into the knit cap I was wearing and stroked my cheek with his thumb.

"Hi," he whispered and kissed me lightly on the lips.

"Hi, yourself," I whispered and kissed him back. "I think Rosalie may be on to us."

"I'm surprised we've fooled them this long, love," he smiled warmly and pulled me in for a deeper kiss. "I've missed you," he murmured against my lips.

"I've missed *you*," I sighed as I threw my leg over his lap and straddled him, running my fingers through his thick hair. My tongue traced the curve of his lips as he grinned while my hips rocked against his lap.

"Little Erik has missed you too," he groaned as he grabbed my ass with both hands and pulled me down with more force against his entrusted body part. The pajama pants he was wearing held nothing back and the friction we were creating felt fabulous. It was all the foreplay we needed. I stood up and shimmied my pants down to my ankles as Erik pulled his down, freeing "Little Erik" to come out and play. I resumed my place awkwardly, but we didn't care. Erik thrust into me as I lowered myself onto him as a "Yes" escaped his mouth and my eyes rolled back into my head.

"Fffffuuucccckkkkk…," I moaned as we moved together. "*God*, you feel good."

"I *am* your god when you ride my dick," he growled and plunged into me with more force.

"Yes!" I hissed as I grabbed fistfuls of his hair again and met his pelvis thrust for thrust.

"Come for me, love," he groaned as he rolled his hips with his next few thrusts causing me to shudder. "I want that wet pussy to come all over my dick." *Fuck.* I felt my orgasm starting to build as we continued our frenzied rhythm.

"*Fuck,* Kelly, I feel it… Come– for– me–," he demanded with each thrust before pouring himself into me with a shudder. My body shook as I gripped his hair tighter and came biting his neck as I moaned his name. *Fuck.*

I half-moaned, half-chuckled as I backed off of Erik's lap and pulled up my pajama pants. Erik reached his arms out for me, his eyes still closed from his orgasm, a sexy smirk on his face.

"Let's go get in bed," I suggested. I grabbed his hands and tried to help him to his feet.

"Too tired," he whined. "Lie down with me here for a bit." It was all the convincing I needed. I laid down on the couch with my legs across Erik's lap as he leaned over, his head against my chest. "Much better," he mumbled, "Don't know why I'm so knackered."

"You have to build up your stamina when you haven't gotten laid for a couple of weeks," I laughed, closing my eyes. Erik didn't respond, so I was afraid he had already fallen asleep. "Erik, you awake?"

"I'm awake," he sighed, sounding more awake than he did just a second ago.

"Is everything okay?" I asked, then it hit me. *I'm an idiot.* "It hasn't been a couple of weeks for you, has it?" I squeezed my eyes shut anticipating his answer.

"Do you really want to know, love?" he asked softly. *No. Yes. No.*

"No, I'm... I'm good," I managed as I got up and walked inside, turning lights off as I went. *This is exactly what you wanted, Kelly.* Erik followed along behind me, not saying a word. "I'll be out in a minute," I told him as I closed the bathroom door. I needed to wrap my brain around this new information. I took my time completing my nighttime regime before opening the door where Erik was still standing, waiting.

"I've used condoms every time," he offered before I was even through the doorway.

"Whoa!" I yelped. My eyes flew open in surprise. "*Every* time. Dang. Okay… Got it." I walked over to the bed and pulled the blankets down to climb in. Erik was still standing, watching me, a look of disbelief on his face.

"I thought this is what you wanted," he gulped, taking a step toward me.

"Oh, it is… it's just tough when reality slaps me in the face. I'll be fine," I breathed and got into bed. *Won't I?*

"If you want me to stop seeing other people, just say it, Kel." I shook my head and pulled up the covers. Erik sat down facing me on the bed and grabbed my hands. The look of sincerity on his face nearly brought tears to my eyes. "Have you changed your mind?" he implored. A wistful smile crossed my face as I placed my hand on his cheek, rubbing the scruff on his jawline that he had been growing out.

"It *is* what I want," I sighed. "I guess I was just being naive to think that I haven't seen anyone so you must not have either." I kissed him lightly on the mouth and kept my hand on his cheek. *Do I need a distraction from my distraction?* "I'm okay. Just caught a little off guard."

"What about Boring Sex Ray? Has he sniffed around?" The nickname made me smile.

"He's persistent," I replied with a chuckle. "I've told him we just needed to be friends, but I don't think he agrees. I'm just not interested."

"Can't say I'm sorry about that," Erik said quietly, while I rolled my eyes. *He* was the one that just confessed to fucking someone. "Rosalie still loves bringing him up."

"I've noticed that," I chuckled. "Are you jealous?" I teased.

Erik shrugged. "Perhaps," he smirked, "But I know he can't please you like I can." He kissed down my neck as he lifted my shirt over my head. "Is there something I can do to please you right now?" he murmured against my breast as he captured my nipple in his mouth and sucked. I groaned in approval, tilting my head back allowing Erik more access to my chest. He tickled my hardened nipple with his tongue as he pinched the other, then gave it a tongue bath like the first. My insides were liquid as I watched him lavish attention on my bare, pale chest.

Erik looked up into my eyes, his nearly black with desire. He turned me on the bed, so I was sitting near the edge. "I'm going to eat this wet pussy," he moaned as he pushed me to lie down. He kissed down my body until he came to the waistband of my pajama pants. Pulling those down, he yanked them off letting them fall to the floor and slid his nose over my wet vaginal lips. "Until you scream my name," he growled and dove in, sucking and licking until I came over and over again.

"Er–ik... Fuck... Er–ik!" I hollered as I came the last time. My bones felt like they were made of rubber as they hung over the bed. He helped pull me up, so my head was back on the pillow, then chuckled as he wiped his face with the back of his hand. I grabbed his hand and brought it to my mouth, licking where he had just wiped it.

"Stay just like that," he moaned as he wrapped his hand around his erect shaft and began pumping it up and down. I batted my eyes at him as I reached up and squeezed my breasts together. I flicked my nipples and moaned as he increased his rhythm, his eyes glazed over with desire. I left one hand on my breast as I reached over with the other and cupped his manhood gently as he jacked off over me. "Fuck," he growled as I reached further and stuck the tip of my finger in his rear. His head flung back as he let out a primitive roar when I slid it in further, exploring as I watched him come undone.

"Come for me," I purred. Erik opened his eyes and watched as he spread his seed all over my naked torso.

"Fuck me... that was hot," Erik laughed when he was able to catch his breath. I laughed too as I tried to get up without touching anything. Thanks to his large load, I was a sticky mess. He bounded off the bed and helped me up.

"I need a warm shower... wanna scrub my back?" I teased.

"As long as you keep your hands to yourself," he groaned. "Vixen..."

"Deal," I laughed. We showered together quickly and crawled back into bed, both of us barely able to keep our eyes open.

"Let me know if you change your mind, will ya?" Erik asked as he wrapped his arms around me, pulling me close to his chest. He squeezed as he kissed the top of my head.

"Change my mind about what?" I asked sleepily. I had no idea what he meant.

"About seeing other people," he murmured. "You might be all that I can handle."

Chapter 28

Larry took Erik and his Assholes up to one of the trailheads early the next morning for their hiking excursion. It was all hands on deck for everyone else I knew to help set up for the Chamber party that evening. The steak, chicken, and veggies were marinating for fajitas and all the sides were prepped with a huge pot of my spicy charro beans stewing on the stove. I guess I could have gone with a more traditional "spring" theme, but I loved any excuse to make Mexican food. The house was a welcoming beacon with party lights aglow, the fuel-filled heaters were lit on the deck while a small band played crowd favorites on the large stone patio to the side as the Chamber guests began to arrive. Before long, the house was filled to the brim with people both inside and out and left me wondering if there could be anyone left in town.

The party was going off without a hitch. Rosalie and her friend Jane (who helped us out on occasion) made sure our serving trays were full, I had hired June and Daryl's daughter to play bartender, Skyler and Sam were mingling amongst the guests, and Larry had brought Erik and his Assholes back from the trailhead a while ago… though I had only seen a glimpse of Erik when they got back.

I was out on the deck, schmoozing with a couple of local real estate investors, when a voice behind me murmured, "Great party."

Disappointment washed over me as I recognized the voice. "Hi Ray," I said, turning towards him. "Thanks! I'm glad you could make it."

"You *do* remember my name," he gasped jokingly, reaching out for a hug. I had told Ray several times since the dinner at his house that I only wanted to be friends, but like I told Erik… he was persistent.

"Ha ha. Very funny," I smiled and turned for a side hug. "How have you been?"

"Good," he smiled and took a drink of his water. Ray, being a two-drink-max kinda guy, always spaced each one out with a glass of water. He really was a nice, straight-laced guy. "Making plans for next year and making sure this one goes as planned. You?"

I returned his smile and nodded. Ray's lavender farm had been featured on a celebrity's social media page, so his busy season had started early… though summer was normally our peak tourist time. "Same. Hoping to get some of the cabins upgraded after the end of next season. Fingers crossed! What do y'all have planned?" Ray launched into a detailed list of improvements he had in the works that kept my interest. Conversation flowed well with Ray and I since we had our tourism businesses in common, so I lost track of how long we stood there and chatted, though I did glance around from time to time hoping to catch a glimpse of Erik. It was only when a couple of my guests came to bid their farewells that I realized the time.

"Ooo, I better go make the rounds. I'll talk to you later, Ray," I smiled and headed inside, keeping an eye out for Erik as I went. Making sure to chat with everyone there, I still had not seen him among the guests. *He's probably hiding out with Larry.* I spied Sam and Skyler inside by the bar and sidled up to check in.

"Y'all having fun?" I asked while keeping my eyes peeled for my dark-haired Englishman.

"Not too bad… we're about to go. Great turnout!" said Sam loudly. I nodded as I kept a lookout around the large space. "Whoya looking for?" she asked smugly. *That got my attention.*

I glanced at Sam with a smirk and took a drink of my cider. "Who do you think?"

"I wasn't sure after seeing how long you talked to that guy out on the deck," she teased, dropping her voice to a whisper. "People seemed excited about it from what we heard in here." Sam watched me over her beer glass as she took a drink.

I rolled my eyes. "That's Boring Sex Ray," I hissed. "People can be excited all they want… it's *not* going to happen."

"The one person *not* excited about it was Erik," Skyler whispered.

I leveled a wide-eyed stare at Sam's girlfriend. "You saw Erik? What do you mean? Did he say something?"

"Let's just say his mood worsened the longer y'all stood there," Sam replied suspiciously.

"Sam may have provoked him a little," Skyler giggled.

"Jealousy can be good sometimes," Sam countered with a grin.

"What did you say? What happened?" I implored, shaking my head. Though a dose of jealousy really could be good for Erik after what I learned last night.

"Take a breath… nothing bad, I promise," Sam swore. "I just mentioned how much you and Ray had in common. He mumbled something about *The Simpsons* and walked off."

"I'm sure he's somewhere with Larry. I need to go talk to some people before they leave. Brunch tomorrow?" We made quick plans for the next day, then I bid the two lovebirds goodnight as I began mingling. My mind wandered to Erik as it did more and more often. *Maybe a little jealousy is good for both of us.*

Slowly but surely, more and more guests said goodnight, then my helpers, until it was only Ray and I left in the entryway. I was surprised that Erik still hadn't made an appearance.

"The food was fantastic. Thanks for a great night," Ray said for the third time as he started to open the door. *Someone's dragging their feet.* "Looks like I'm the last one here. If you'd like, I could stay and go over some more ideas I had for our farms," Ray said eagerly.

"Tonight's not a good night, mate." That stupid, sexy voice sent shivers down my body every time. I wheeled around to see Erik leaning against the hallway door behind me whirling an amber-colored liquid in his cocktail glass. He was barefoot, wearing my favorite tight, white T-shirt and low-slung workout pants. *Fuck, he looked good.*

"Sorry, I didn't realize you had company," Ray sheepishly replied.

"Well, technically, I always have company," I joked, trying to ease the tension. "Ray this is Erik. I don't think y'all have met before."

"Oh yeah," Ray nodded in recognition, "your late husband's friend."

"I'm Kelly's friend too," Erik replied casually. *Awkward.*

"Yep," I smiled and clapped my hands nervously, "my friend too. Well, good night, Ray," I said and started reaching behind him for the door.

"Would you like to stay and have a drink with us?" Erik's voice was deceptively sweet. "Any friend of Kelly's is a friend of mine," he smiled and held his drink up like he was giving a toast. I rolled my eyes and flipped him off while Ray's attention was focused on Erik.

"Oh no, I better not," smiled Ray, waving his arms. "I've already reached my two-drink limit. Thanks for the invitation, though." I opened the door wider and patted his shoulder.

"Good night, Ray. We'll talk soon about those plans." I smiled as he walked out the door.

"Good night, Kelly. Nice to meet you, Erik," Ray smiled back and headed toward his car. Erik walked up and stood next to me silently in the doorway as Ray pulled out of the driveway. He reached down, grabbed my hand and pulled me back inside.

"Follow me," he murmured as we walked through the house. Erik stopped when we got to the deck, turned around and crushed his mouth to mine. His tongue darted around my tongue then probed further wanting more. His hands were in my hair, fisting it to pull me closer. I could taste the bourbon from his drink on his tongue.

"I want to fuck you right here," he moaned, "right where I had to watch you talk to that boring bloke all night." *Fuck, this is hot.*

Pulling a chair closer, I faced away from Erik then looked back at him over my shoulder. "Is this where I was?" I asked innocently as I bent over and rubbed my ass against Erik's crotch.

"Vixen," he groaned as he grabbed my hips and ground against me. "Is your pussy wet for me?" he moaned in my ear. He unfastened my jeans and slid his fingers inside. "Yes…," he hissed as his finger slipped inside my wet lips making me buck against him.

"Did Boring Ray ever get your pussy this wet?" I could only shake my head as Erik slid his finger out of me then slid two back in making me groan. "Fuck, Kel," he murmured as he moved his fingers faster and faster, finger-fucking me as I groaned his name. He pulled out of me long enough to push my pants down and bend me over the chair. He squatted down behind me and ran his tongue up my center, licking and sucking my clit, then tonguing my ass as he continued his path.

"Whose tongue do you want, vixen?" He grunted as his tongue continued its assault.

"Yours," I managed to breathe out. He yanked down his pants and rubbed his shaft against my wet opening, teasing me with his tip, making me pant with need.

"Whose dick do you want, vixen?" he growled, taunting me again with the head of his hard staff, barely sliding in then pulling it back out.

"Yours," I cried, pushing back against him.

"Damn right," he bellowed as he sunk into me, making me catch my breath. He filled me completely and the relief was glorious.

"Fuck me," I pleaded, pushing against him.

"Ab– so– lutely," Erik thrust forcefully with each syllable. He ran his hand down my back then reached down and eased his thumb into my asshole. The sensation was foreign at first, but I relaxed the more Erik thrust his magnificent dick inside me. *Fuck me!*

I felt my orgasm building the more he pounded. "Here I come," I yelled as I gave in and fell over into the orgasmic abyss.

"Fuck yeah!" Erik cried as he followed me into the depth. We collapsed onto one of the lounge chairs panting and exhausted.

I could not find a comfortable position once Erik and I finally made it to bed. After tossing and turning until the wee hours of the morning, I decided a different course of action was needed. *Weed and the hot tub.* Sinking into the hot water, I felt my muscles instantly relax as I lit my water bong and enjoyed my developing high. Hearing the sliding door open a little later made me giggle, being I was as high as a dang kite.

"Could you not sleep, love?" Erik asked with concern as he walked towards me wearing only his jogging pants slung low on his hips. His nipples were standing erect against the cold, night air.

"Fuck, you look good," I smirked. Throwing my head back with laughter, I handed Erik my bong. "Whoops! I didn't mean to say that out loud," I professed. Erik shook his head while he lit what was left in the bong.

"Shit," he said exhaling, "no wonder you're looped."

"It's good stuff," I giggled and laid my head back against the headrest of the tub. "So... are we going to *talk* about what happened earlier?" I asked after a few quiet minutes.

"Not sorry about your arsehole, love," he smiled. "You didn't ask before you explored mine... I was returning the favor." Erik leaned over and bit my exposed shoulder. I giggled then shook my head.

"I was talking about the Ray stuff, silly," I sighed with exasperation.

"Ned Flanders?" Erik laughed. "You have your very own Ned fucking Flanders." I could appreciate the reference, but I wasn't in the mood. "He's the neighbor from *The Simpsons*." He explained slowly and looked at me like I had grown two heads. I rolled my eyes.

"I know who Ned Flanders is. I meant the whole… 'Tonight's not a good night, mate'," I exaggerated his English accent as I mimicked what he said to Ray. "Was that necessary?"

He shrugged, "What? It wasn't a good night."

"Then you asked him if he wanted to stay for a drink." I raised my eyebrows in question.

"I was being polite," he shrugged again. I looked at him while I waited for him to continue. "Why is everyone *obsessed* with this Ray bloke?" he finally asked.

"Obsessed? Who's *obsessed*?" I narrowed my eyes skeptically.

"Rosalie, Sam and all your friends. Your townspeople wouldn't stop prattling on about him." Erik stood and hitched his pants up as he began pacing back and forth, obviously agitated.

"He's a nice guy, attractive, and we have our businesses in common," I shrugged. "That's who people think I should fit with." Erik stopped his pacing and looked at me with concentration before sitting back down on the edge of the tub.

"But *you* don't." His eyes searched mine for understanding.

"But I don't."

"Can't they see that you fit with me?" he asked earnestly. He placed both hands on my face and drew me in, kissing me softly over and over.

"I don't think they see that," I smiled wistfully as he continued kissing my face. Erik leaned back enough to look into my eyes.

"How could they not?" His sincerity was humbling. I kissed him sweetly, running my tongue along his lips and touching the tip of his tongue with mine.

"Because why would a hot, *muscley*, younger man like you be interested in an older," I quirked an eyebrow, "*less-fit,* pothead like me?" I smiled. "I'm not normally one to down myself, but you have to admit it's a stretch." Erik looked at me with confusion before shaking his head.

"You shallow, fucker," he laughed, my eyes widened in surprise. "Have I ever told you what gave me my first real hard-on?" I shook my head, having no idea where he was going with this story. "I was on a school holiday at an art museum in London, when a woman in a painting I saw made me stop and stare and," he saluted mockingly, "ships ahoy!" I chuckled along with him. "It was called *Samson and Delilah,*" he smiled as he reminisced. "Sure, her knockers were out," he laughed, "but I thought she was soft, curvy, and beautiful… You reminded me of her the first time that night you, your friend and I were in this hot tub."

I thought back to that night, the night I felt a shift in our relationship, the way he was looking at me. I made a mental note to Google that painting.

"My own fucking wet dream come to life," he continued, as he raked his thumb across my lips, his eyes were dark pools of desire. I bit down on his thumb when he swiped it back across my mouth making him groan. "Vixen," he growled, "This– this– friends with benefit shit is not working for me," he blurted looking up at the roof of the pergola. My stomach dropped and my eyes welled with tears. I was completely caught off guard. I knew that this wouldn't last forever, but I didn't plan on it ending so soon.

Erik looked back down and saw the tears threatening to spill over. With a flash of alarm, he climbed into the hot tub next to me splashing water over the sides and captured my face in his hands, kissing the tears that then began to fall.

"No, no, no love. It's not like that. I'm sorry. I'm sorry," he murmured as he feathered kisses all over my cheeks. "What I mean, what I mean is…" he took a deep breath. "I want to walk up and not have to look around before I kiss you. I want to sit at a party and hold your hand no matter who is there." He picked up my hand and kissed it gently. "I wanted the people at your party to be talking about you and me out on this deck… not you and bloody Ned Flanders." There was a yearning when he looked into my eyes. "When we're together, I want us to be *together*," he professed.

I took a deep breath as I peered into his warm, brown eyes. "I want that too…" holding up a finger when he tried to interrupt, "when we're together." Erik groaned and rolled his eyes.

"You're mine every other weekend," he resolved. "Why do we need to see anyone else?"

"We don't *have* to see anyone else, but we can if we want. What's the rush?" I asked, inching closer. "We're taking a step forward, why not leave it at that for now?" I leaned in closer and kissed him. "I just don't want either one of us to have regrets later," I sighed as I dipped my tongue between his lips.

"Just to be clear," Erik leaned back, away from my deepening kiss. "I can walk in next time and kiss you hello… no matter the circumstance?" He tilted his head giving me a half smirk.

"Absolutely," I grinned and continued my exploration of his mouth.

Sam and Skyler swung by late the next morning for brunch, just missing Erik who had left for a hike with his Assholes. Eyeing Erik's drying pants on the railing by the hot tub, Sam lifted an eyebrow. "Do I even want to know?" she asked.

I laughed out loud. "I had a hard time sleeping last night," I shrugged, "and Erik helped me sort– it– out!" I pumped up my fists with each word.

Sam held up a finger and wagged her other finger over it making Skyler giggle. "Gross! Here's the line and you crossed it, sister," Sam gasped teasingly, then turned her smile to Skyler who was still laughing at her joke.

"Y'all are too cute," I beamed, looking at the two of them smiling at one another with damn near hearts in their eyes.

"Hell yeah, we are," Sam sighed, still looking at Skyler. "Now we want to hear about *you*," she mumbled as she turned and stuffed a large bite of her crepe into her mouth. *Where to start?*

"Well…" I began. "Erik and I decided last night that we're not going to hide our relationship anymore," Sam started to interrupt, but I put my finger up knowing what she was going to ask. "Yes, we are still seeing other people," I took a drink of my coffee. "At least *he* is," I blanched.

"He told you he was seeing someone?" Skyler gasped with her eyes open wide. Sam's eyes were just as wide as she held her fork in midair. I shook my head.

"It was my fault," I admitted. "I screwed up and made a stupid joke, assuming he hadn't seen anyone since I hadn't," I shrugged and took another drink. "I can't get upset. He's doing exactly what I asked him to do." *Remember that, Kelly.*

"Being open about your relationship sounds like it's getting more serious," Sam stated skeptically. I nodded and told them about our conversation in the hot tub the night before. "What the hell, Kelly?" Sam asked irritably. "What's this painting? Have you looked it up?"

I pulled up the picture of the painting that I had found on my phone and passed it over to Sam and Skyler. I didn't think it looked much like me, except for the shape of the woman. Sam looked up at me with confusion, as she began to lecture. "He likes curvy women, since that's what horned him up for the first time. He wants to be with you, here, where you both love it. You got upset when you thought he was going to end it," she threw up her arms again. "What am I missing? Why are you not stamping 'Property of Kelly' on Erik's ass and calling it a day?"

"I was with the same man for nearly thirty years. I'm not ready to settle down with another just yet… no matter how sexy… fun… smart… good in bed…" I drifted off as I took another sip of my coffee and smiled dreamily, remembering how good Erik looked that morning waking up. Sam and Skyler's matching looks of disbelief made me chuckle when I glanced up. "What's the rush?" I conceded. "There's no biological clock ticking in the background."

Sam pointed her fork at me as she replied. "What happens if someone else snags Loverboy's attention while you're gallivanting around?"

She spoke my biggest fear aloud, at least when it came to Erik. "Then it was fun while it lasted, I guess…though the thought makes me want to puke," I moaned and pretended to gag. "But I'm not going to commit before I'm ready just because I'm scared Erik might find someone else to fall in love with. I just want us both to be happy. Besides… I might need to have my options open later this spring," I hinted, wiggling my brow suggestively.

"What's happening later this spring?" Skyler giggled.

"*Someone* made a reservation here with a few of his friends from Texas," I taunted, but Sam was not that interested in my theatrics.

"I have no idea," she responded nonchalantly and handed her plate to Skyler for another crepe, smiling as their hands met. *Sam will be living here within a year.* I smiled at the thought, then got back to the matter at hand.

"It's no big deal," I said, wiping my mouth as I stood up from the table. "Just a little someone by the name of Sam fucking Walker!" I yelled so loudly it echoed across the valley. Sam's fork fell to her plate as her mouth hung open in disbelief. Skyler looked from one of us to the other trying to decipher what was happening. Sam was finally able to speak.

"Sam fucking Walker?" she asked, wide-eyed, as I nodded, glad to see that her interest was now piqued. "The *same* Sam Walker that you've been in love with since the eighth grade? *That* Sam Walker?"

"That's the one," I laughed as Sam still stared at me wide-eyed.

"The *same* Sam Walker that you saved your virginity for until you were twenty, since you just *knew* that y'all would be together? *That* Sam fucking Walker?" She asked again even louder, standing up out of her chair.

I laughed thinking back to those years. I really did think we were meant to be together, though he never saw me that way. "The one and only," I smiled smugly, pointing my finger pistols at her as I spoke.

"The *same* Sam Walker whose wife posted on social media a while back that they're getting divorced? *That* Sam Walker?" Sam hollered as she threw her napkin down on the table. "Holy shit," she sighed as she sat back down and took a deep breath. I turned down the deck heater and resumed my seat, suddenly feeling flushed.

"I saw his mother when I was back in Texas over the holidays, and she told me about the divorce. I suggested a guys' fishing trip up here, and he grabbed one of our last open reservations a few weeks ago," I chuckled. "We've been sending flirty emails back and forth, so I guess we'll just see what happens." Sam eyed me with a shrewd smirk as I shrugged my shoulders, grabbed my phone and started scrolling.

"If anyone could give Erik a run for their money on your lady parts, it would be Sam Walker," she stated then turned toward Skyler. "Kelly was in *love* with this guy for *so* long, but he never reciprocated her affection," she explained.

"Here's a recent pic that he sent me," I handed Sam my phone so she could assess the smoke show for herself. His blue eyes were still as bright as I remember. "Our parents were really good friends growing up, so we spent a lot of time together," I said to Skyler as Sam inspected the picture. "I was just the chubby family friend with no boundaries and zero fashion sense," I shrugged. "I just always thought we would be so perfect for one another, and one day he would wake up and realize it too." I chuckled to myself as I sipped my coffee, thinking back to how sure I was that we would be together.

"He still looks good," sighed Sam as she handed me back the phone. "A little thicker around the middle, but good. So you're wanting to keep your options open with Erik in case you get your chance with Sam Walker?"

"Uh, hello... I had no idea Sam Walker was even available until a few months ago," I said knowingly, "But yeah, kinda. At least I could say yes if he tried something." I laughed remembering how awkward he was around girls back when we were young. I guess he didn't need any moves when he was *that* good-looking. "Or *I* could try something with him," I muttered. "What do I have to lose?"

"Girl!" Sam exclaimed. "If you are getting flirty vibes from Sam Walker when he is here, then you *better* try something!" She sat on the edge of her chair as she jabbed her finger at me. "I don't want to have to listen to your wails of regret for the rest of our lives if you don't!" *She really does know me well.*

"Deal," I reassured, laughing at the doubtful expression on Sam's face, "I promise!" She seemed to be satisfied with that response as she sat back in her chair.

"Anything else we need to know?" asked Skyler. Sam smiled over at her like she was the best thing ever. It would almost be enough to make me gag if I wasn't so excited for Sam.

"Not quite as thrilling as the rest of my news," I admitted, "but I'm going with Lindsey and the girls to a ranch in Montana to celebrate Lindsey's divorce. Want to see if I can bring a plus two?" I pleaded playfully. I knew that Sam wouldn't be interested in either the ranch or a week with my friends.

"Thanks, but no thanks," she quipped as she stood up to help me clear off the remnants of our brunch. "When are y'all going?"

"In a few weeks," I said as I walked into the kitchen and began cleaning up. Skyler and Sam followed behind with the remainder of our dishes then sat at the kitchen island to finish their coffee. "The girls are flying up, but I'm driving over. Should be a fun trip."

"That's all you," Sam laughed. "I'm sure y'all will have a good time. How's Lindsey doing?"

"She's doing well," I smiled. "It seems like so many of us are starting over… or maybe I should say starting new chapters in our lives," I said looking over at Sam and Skyler smiling at one another. "It's fun to see what directions we'll take," I added, though I wasn't sure if they were even listening to me at that point.

I finished cleaning the kitchen while Sam and Skyler talked about their summer plans. I was excited to see their relationship progressing, especially if it meant there was a chance Sam would move here. "You'll have to put up with seeing me more, Kelly," Sam snickered. I would have done a backflip if I could.

"I think I could manage," I laughed. "Y'all wanna stay for dinner? I've got stuff for lasagna…" I coaxed, "and garlic cheese bread." The way to Sam's heart was always through her stomach.

"You had *me* at lasagna," Skyler giggled and looked at Sam who threw her arms up in mock surrender.

"I can't argue with that," she laughed. "We'll run home and grab better wine and come back around six o'clock. Will that work?" I giggled to myself with Sam's use of the word "home".

"Can't argue with that either. Larry should be back with Erik and his Assholes, but only Erik will stay for dinner," I said, thinking out loud. "I'll invite Larry and Rosalie and Daryl and June over too. How does that sound?"

Sam and Skyler agreed and left in search of the better wine while I got to work prepping dinner. A few hours later, the lasagna was in the oven and the salad was prepped, all I needed were hungry people. The googly-eyed lovers were the first ones back with enough wine for the whole hillside.

"We're staying the night," Sam laughed as she uncorked a bottle. "Hope you don't mind," she smiled artificially as I giggled. Rosalie was the next one to arrive, with Daryl and June following close behind. Erik texted that they would be there in ten minutes. *Perfect timing.* My stomach did a backflip with anticipation. I already had the patio heaters on, since we would dine al fresco for the first time that season. The deck was inviting after the cold months of winter. Skyler poured a round of wine for all of us as we nibbled on cheese and crackers that I had laid on the table, while Rosalie entertained us with the latest drama between her and my grumpy property manager. The driveway alarm chimed meaning Larry and Erik were back, and my heart skipped a beat.

"They'll probably want to have a drink or two before we eat," I stood to grab another bottle of wine, when we heard the front door close and heavy footsteps trodding through the house. Larry and Erik joined us on the deck, and I returned Erik's smile when our eyes locked. I glanced down at his loose cargo pants and forest green Henley that made him look like an ad for L.L. Bean. My eyes journeyed upward again and met his devilish smirk as he walked towards me. My heart was beating a mile a minute as he got closer. Stopping in front of me, he reached up and placed his hands on my face as he pulled me in for a firm yet passionate kiss. *What the–?*

"Hello," he murmured. *I can walk in next time and kiss you hello.* My eyes cut sideways to see Rosalie's eyes as big as pie plates then over to Larry's who were more like quarters, though that was big for Larry. Daryl and June were silent, but both had huge smiles on their faces. Rosalie took an audible deep breath.

"Ooo," she howled, "Larry owes me twenty bucks!" she laughed as she took a big swig of her wine. "I just *knew* you'd get together."

271

"Yep, I didn't think so. I figured you were too old for him," Larry grunted and reached for his wine glass not seeming to be bothered much by what just transpired.

"Fuck you, Larry! How much older are you than Rosalie?" I yelped, throwing a napkin at him. He grinned widely showing two of his missing teeth. He must have forgotten to put his new ones in on his rush to pick up Erik.

"The older the berry, the sweeter the juice!" he crooned, then laughed hysterically at his own joke.

"I don't think that's how the saying goes, you toothless bastard," I laughed as Larry shrugged and drank his wine. Sam, Skyler and Rosalie were wiping their eyes from tears of laughter, while Daryl and June hugged me tight. Erik just shook and bowed his head then took his turn hugging the neighbors. Never a dull moment with this crew.

Chapter 29

"I guess we didn't have to worry about our friends around here," I said as I walked Erik to his SUV that next evening. He had decided to take the day off and spend it with me completing odd jobs around the farm, while Larry took a couple of days off to spend with Rosalie. I had never had so much fun repairing fence and shoveling shit.

"Were you worried?" Erik asked, throwing his bag in the backseat.

"No, they all love this kind of crap. I'm sure I'll get a ton more questions once they have time to stew on it," I smiled. "Be careful driving back, it's already gotten so dark." Erik pulled me into his arms and kissed me soundly.

"I will," he smiled and kissed me again. "I'll miss you," he sighed as he climbed in his vehicle.

"I'll miss *you*," I whispered as I rubbed his leg while he adjusted his seat to prepare for the drive. I wasn't ready for him to go. *Would he have another date?* I shook my head to clear it from the direction of my thoughts.

"You alright, love?" Erik asked as he tipped my chin up to meet his worried stare. My breath caught at the tenderness I saw looking back at me. I placed my hands on his face and pulled him towards me, kissing him passionately as he moaned in response. I deepened the kiss, fucking his mouth with my tongue as I entwined my fingers in his hair. I heard a whirring sound as his driver's seat started to move away from the steering wheel and recline. Smiling as I taunted him with my tongue, I slid my hand down his chest and towards the waist of his jeans.

"Hang on, vixen," Erik purred as he took a minute to look around. He then unfastened his jeans and pushed them down to his knees along with his boxer briefs. "Take your pants off and climb on," he invited seductively. My eyes grew wide as I looked all around. Larry was in town at Rosalie's and Erik's SUV was parked between the house and the barn, not in sight of the cabins and especially private with it growing dark. I didn't break eye contact as I kicked off my sandals and slid my pants down quickly. I climbed onto Erik's lap as he closed the door, then I immediately began to laugh.

"You do know my perfectly good bed is just inside, right?" I moaned as Erik slid his thumb into my womanhood. I rocked against him, moaning louder.

"Where's the fun in that?" he murmured against my neck as I ground against him. He pulled his hand away and grabbed my hips as he plunged his full length into my core. I gasped from the sensation as he pulled back and embedded himself again to the hilt. "Fuck," he groaned, as I circled my hips and ground against him as he continued thrusting. Movement was a little tough within the confines of his driver's seat, but we seemed to be figuring it out. "Take this bloody thing off," he murmured as he pushed up my shirt. I pulled it over my head as he brought his face down within my cleavage and bit down.

"Ow," I gasped as he chuckled.

"Just wanted to give you a souvenir," he panted and smiled wickedly. *Bastard.*

"I need to turn around," I groaned, partly because my legs were going numb. Erik pulled out and helped me turn around, so I was facing the steering wheel. He pulled me down on his shaft and hissed when he was fully sheathed. "Fuck yeah!" I hollered. *Much better.*

"Damn," he moaned, "*So* deep." He reached around and cupped my breasts in his hands as he began to thrust again. I was able to use my legs more in this position to match his rhythm. "*Yes,* vixen," he growled, circling his hips as he ground into me. *Heaven.*

"I'm... I'm..." I gasped, unable to finish my statement as my eyes rolled back, and I clutched the steering wheel.

"*Yes,* vixen..." Erik coerced, grinding his hips again in that sinful way.

"Fuuuuccccckkk," I wailed as my orgasm gripped my body, which was what he needed to follow me over the edge.

"Fuck me," Erik groaned as he caught his breath and adjusted our position, "I'm going to get a hard-on every time I climb in this bloody thing." Laughing, I tried to move but my legs were done.

"I'm afraid I'll have to sleep right here," I murmured as I placed my head on the steering wheel and closed my eyes. Erik began massaging my back as I groaned loudly, his strong grip from cycling and kayaking made my worked-up muscles melt. "Why don't you stay another night?" I asked, still not looking up. "Just get up early in the morning and leave, since it's already so dark," I appealed. Wildlife was abundant on the Peninsula, so one had to be especially careful driving after dark.

Erik kissed my back as he continued massaging down my arms. "Alright, but..." he kissed my back a few more times, "no hanky panky," he teased, "at least not tonight."

"Deal," I laughed as I opened the door and eased off his lap. We decided to lay in bed and watch a movie as we walked inside. Erik flopped onto the bed and busied himself with finding something for us to watch while I went to the bathroom to get ready for bed. I glanced in the mirror as I took my shirt off and let out a loud gasp. "Erik," I called.

"Yes, my love?" he asked as he leaned against the threshold of the bathroom door and smiled. "I found a movie for us to..." he trailed off as his eyes wandered down to my chest. "Shit!" Erik's eyes widened as he saw the huge bruise that he had left on my breast. "I said I would leave a souvenir, but I must have gotten a little carried away," he smiled with repentance.

"Really?" I laughed in disbelief, "a *little* carried away?" A bit of an understatement considering the bruise was about two inches in diameter. "I don't even remember the last time I had a hickey," I laughed again, shaking my head.

Erik walked over to me and brushed the darkening bruise lightly with his finger. "I would say I won't do it again," he looked into my eyes and smirked, "but I won't make a promise I don't intend to keep." He kissed me loudly and laughed, leaning back against the bathroom counter.

"Maybe I should return the favor," I smiled with phony innocence. *Explain THAT to another woman.*

"Go ahead," Erik murmured, leaning down and kissing the bruise he left on my chest. My eyebrows shot up in surprise. *That* was not the answer I was anticipating. He looked into my eyes with expectation along with his sexiest smirk.

"Where?" I asked, matching his smirk with my own. He would probably say somewhere inconspicuous, but I was not going to back down.

Erik leaned his head to the side and pointed at his neck. "We'll go old school," he winked. My eyes widened, shocked by his suggestion. *Did he think I would say no?*

I narrowed my eyes and looked at him with uncertainty. "Aren't you afraid someone will see?" I asked with the same sugary, sweet tone. "I wouldn't want to *throw shade* on your *game,*" I laughed as I wiggled my eyebrows. Erik rolled his eyes as he leaned forward and kissed me again.

"My *game* is just fine," he chuckled. "C'mon…" he coaxed, "I want a souvenir, too." He rubbed his neck against my face, like a cat requesting attention, making me laugh out loud.

"I don't think I can," I giggled. "I can't concentrate." Erik stopped his nudging and walked behind me, so we both faced the bathroom mirror. He reached around and pulled the cups of my bra down so my breasts spilled out into his large, strong hands. He leaned down without breaking eye contact and murmured in my ear.

"In a couple of days, when your bruise starts to fade," he breathed. "I want you to stand right here and touch yourself and think of my mouth on you."

Goosebumps spread out across my arms and my nipples stood erect causing a shiver to run through me. "Then I'll stand in front of my mirror, rub my cock," he continued, "and think of your mouth on me." His eyes smoldered as our eyes held in the reflection of the mirror.

Hot. I turned around and kissed his neck, low against where the collar of his shirt rested. Erik moaned and pulled me closer as I pulled his shirt lower, trailing kisses after it until I found the perfect spot. I nipped at his skin, kissed, then bit his flesh and sucked it into my mouth as he groaned again. After a couple of minutes, I pulled back and giggled at the red welp that had appeared on his lower neck. "Happy?" I smirked and lightly wiped the corners of my lips like I had enjoyed a tasty bite. Erik laughed as he studied himself in the mirror.

"That'll do, vixen," he chuckled and swatted my ass then adjusted himself as he walked into the bedroom. "Still up for a movie?" he called.

"Absolutely," I said aloud as I inspected my hickey in the mirror. I ran my finger around the bruise gently as I thought about what Erik said we'd do in a couple of days. "Absolutely," I whispered again softly and smiled.

Larry was impressed with our work as he and I walked around and inspected our repairs the next morning. Erik had gotten up extra early that morning to head back to Seattle, and I already missed his company.

"I'm happy to see the place didn't fall apart without me," Larry laughed as I showed him our last patch job on the fence.

"Erik was a good helper," I smiled and giggled thinking about something he had said to one of the goats when it was a little too excited to see us ("buy me dinner first, mate!"). Larry had stopped his inspection of the fence and was surveying *me,* instead, with a look of amusement.

"I bet he was," he laughed. "Erik made Rosy's day with his little show of affection the other day. She had the two of you figured out a long time ago."

"I shouldn't be surprised. Sorry I kept it from you," I added sheepishly. "We're just keeping it casual." We were quiet for a few minutes as we watched the pigs root around in their muddy sty. "What do you really think of us being together?"

Larry kept staring out at the pigs for so long I wondered if he heard me, before he took a sip of his coffee and turned toward me. "Honestly?" he asked, which caused me to gulp in fear as I nodded my head. "I think it's great. And... for what it's worth... I think Jake would be thrilled that you and Erik found comfort with each other. Hell, Kelly. He was such a planner that he probably orchestrated the whole goddamn thing." *Son of a bitch.* The snippet of Jake and Erik's conversation that I overheard that night on the deck flashed through my memory. Larry was probably right; Jake was still looking out for me.

"Thanks, Larry. I'm happy that you're on board," I smiled.

"I'm on board for whatever you have planned, my sister from another mister," he grinned widely, showing that he had forgotten to put his teeth in. I rolled my eyes and turned away as he died laughing and grabbed his teeth from the pocket of his shirt and slid them back into place.

"Larry!" I groaned knowing where his nasty hands had been and laughed at the ridiculousness of some of the people in my life.

Chapter 30

"Why is no one picking up?" I said aloud, hanging up the phone as Sam's voicemail recording started playing. Erik hadn't answered either, and I was driving east across the Peninsula headed to Seattle for a pit stop at his place, before continuing to Montana for Lindsey's Divorce Extravaganza. The girls and I were spending a week at a dude ranch outside of Bozeman, but they were flying, and I was road-tripping since it was only a ten-hour drive from Seattle. My phone rang across my car speakers, as Sam called me back.

"Hey woman, did you get my message?" I asked, answering the call.

"I did. Sorry I forgot that you wouldn't be home this weekend," Sam answered. She had texted saying she was coming into town for a quick visit with Skyler. I was going to miss both her visit and Erik's weekend for this divorce party, so I hoped this ranch was going to be as fun as Lindsey made it seem.

"It's okay. I'm sure you'll be back up again soon," I chuckled. "I'm on my way to Seattle now to see Erik and stay over before driving to Montana tomorrow. It might end up being a surprise though, since he hasn't answered my calls or texts."

"He doesn't know you're coming over?" she asked in surprise. I wasn't normally one to just pop in without warning.

"Not really. We had been planning on it, then I told him earlier this week that I wasn't going to be able to swing it. But… I got everything done, so I'm heading there now." I checked the time and decided I would try Erik again after my phone call with Sam. "I really wanted to see him, since I won't get to see him this weekend," I whined. "He came over for an extra-long visit the last time, and neither of us were ready for him to leave." I left out the incredible phone sex we had a few days later, just like Erik had described the night in the bathroom.

Sam laughed. "Do you even hear yourself right now?"

"What do you mean?" I asked, paying more attention to the road than to my train of thought.

"Y'all are in *love*," she drew out the last word with exasperation.

"Wh– What?" I stammered, a little louder than needed.

Sam enunciated each word slowly like I was unable to hear. "You're in love with him, Kel. And he's in love with you too." She sighed loudly. "I don't think even Sam Walker could change that."

I let out a deep breath. I hated it when Sam was right. "Maybe you're right," I said quietly.

"Oh honey, I *know* I am," she laughed.

"Fuck you," I chuckled. "I'll talk to him tonight and let you know what happens. I have a ten-hour drive tomorrow, so call me."

"Yea! It's about damn time," she cheered. "I'll call you tomorrow. Good luck! I want *all* the details."

"Maybe not *all* the details," I laughed, "but I'll let you know. Talk to you tomorrow!" The call ended as I still laughed to myself. *I'm in love with Erik.* I tried calling him again, but the call went to voicemail. I sent another text once I got onto the ferry, but I still had not heard from him when I pulled into the parking garage of his building and saw his SUV parked in his assigned spot.

I sat parked for a while contemplating what I should do. Erik had surprised me at the farm before when Lindsey and the girls were visiting, so he had set the precedent. I decided I would leave my overnight bag in my jeep and knock on his door. Butterflies fluttered in my stomach as I watched the numbers increase on the elevator creeping closer to his floor. *Maybe I should just say it when he opens the door. Rip the bandaid off.* I got to his floor and walked to his door. Taking a deep breath, I rang the bell. *Breathe, Kelly.* The door opened and I nearly choked on the breath I was holding. I glanced at the number by the apartment door then back at the gorgeous brunette that had just opened the door. *Fuck.*

"Can I help you?" she asked. I looked again at the number by the door of the apartment then back to the beautiful stranger who answered Erik's door.

"Is Erik here?" I asked hesitantly.

"He's in the shower," she said with a dazzling smile. "He should be out in a minute if you want to wait." The supermodel looked more like a real estate agent opening the door wider to welcome me inside. I walked in, feeling slightly self-conscious as I looked down at my jeans and flip flops. Not wanting to intrude any further, I stopped in the entry. *Good thing I'm not a psycho killer.*

"I'll wait right here," I smiled cordially and took a deep breath when she walked into the other room. *Fuck. Should I leave?* My eyes grew misty as I looked at the framed pictures of smiling faces around Erik's entryway, resting on one of my favorites of him and Jake that I had given him a while back. The one next to it caught my eye… it was Erik and I at the gala last year. I picked up the frame to get a closer look, having not seen this one before. Erik had given me a framed picture of the two of us from that night, but it was a traditional pose with us smiling at the camera. This one was of Erik, staring at me with the warmest look in his dark, narrowed eyes, giving me his sexiest smirk as my head was thrown back in laughter, our arms wrapped around one another. It was a lovely candid shot, and I thought it perfectly summed up the two of us.

"Who was at the door, love?" Erik called. *Love?* I placed the picture hastily back on the shelf and took a deep breath. Erik stopped when he saw me in his entry, eyes wide with shock. The "love" to whom he was referring joined us in the cramped space.

"Oh, sorry! I didn't even ask your name," she fluttered, placing her hand on my arm. I suddenly felt like I couldn't breathe. The three of us were crammed into this entryway, and there was not enough oxygen for us all.

"Kel," Erik murmured. I put my hand up to stop him, shook my head, and reached for the doorknob. Erik placed his hand on mine. "Give us a minute," he said to the stunner as she shrugged and walked back into the living room. He opened the front door and motioned for me to follow him into the outside hallway. "I'm so sorry," he said as soon as the door closed. He turned to face me and placed both hands on my shoulders. I was already shaking my head, my eyes closed, trying my best to hold the tears at bay. "She's just–"

"It's my fault," I whispered, a few tears slipped through my tightly closed eyes. *Dammit.* "I called and texted, but I should have waited for you to reply." I wiped my eyes with my fingertips avoiding Erik's stare. I felt so stupid putting us in this situation.

"My phone stopped working," he appealed quickly, "So I had to drop it off at a repair shop down the street." Erik tilted my chin up to look him in the eye. "I'm so sorry, my love," he murmured as he wiped my tears with his thumbs. I winced at his last word, remembering he said the same thing to the brunette bombshell just minutes earlier.

"It's what I wanted, remember?" I smiled, but I was sure my eyes showed the despondency I felt. *I'm an idiot for letting my guard down.* I shook my head again and turned toward the elevator. "Enjoy your date. She's gorgeous," I said over my shoulder as I hit the call button for the elevator.

"Wait!" Erik cried, grabbing my arm as I started to walk through the elevator door. "Please come back… later," he groaned.

I gave him a sympathetic smile. "I will in a week," I sighed and hit the button for the elevator again, since it had come and gone.

"On your way back from Montana?" Erik asked.

I nodded. "I'll make sure I talk to you first before dropping by," I smirked, trying to lighten the mood. The elevator was taking its sweet time coming back to our floor.

"Wait… are you driving to Montana *now*?" Erik's voice rose as he spoke.

"I've got a motel room a few hours away as a backup," I lied convincingly. My answer seemed to satisfy Erik's worry. I would set my GPS toward the ranch in Montana and find a place along the way to stop and stay. The elevator signaled its arrival, and I stepped inside. "Try not to miss me too much this weekend," I couldn't read Erik's expression as he stared at me without saying a word. I smiled and winked, trying to cover up the heaviness that I felt in my chest. "Oh shit, whoops!" I forgot that I hadn't chosen a floor, so I hit the button just as Erik stepped onto the elevator. He captured my face in his hands as his lips met mine, nearly taking my breath away.

"I… I…," Erik started but was unable to continue as his dark eyes penetrated my soul. He shook his head, "Not now, not here," he yearned. We stood and stared at one another the few seconds it took before the elevator opened to the lobby. "Let me know when you get to your destination," he sighed into my hair. "Unless you've changed your mind and want to stay here?"

"I'm not into threesomes, remember?" I teased as he groaned. "Go back to your date, Casanova. I'm a big girl... I'll be okay." *Eventually.* I kissed him gently on the lips then walked out of the elevator, letting the doors close. I was barely out of the parking garage when I let the tears rip. *What the fuck, Kelly?* I pulled over in a restaurant parking lot to compose myself. I took some deep breaths and closed my eyes. All I could see were the pearly whites of the cover girl smile that brunette bitch gave me when she opened the door. *Whoa... easy ol' girl. Don't be mad at her just because you're mad at yourself.* I took another deep breath and let out a scream from the depths of my gut, until no more noise came out. *That helped.* Needing a different perspective, I plugged the Montana address for the ranch into the map application on my phone, pulled back onto the highway, and called Sam. She answered right away, her voice bellowing through the speakers of my jeep.

"Hey! I wasn't expecting to hear from you until tomorrow," Sam said by way of a greeting. I gave a recount of what just happened at Erik's. "Fuck me," she said. "How do you feel?"

"Like an idiot," I said, rolling my eyes. "It's a sign that I just need to keep things the way they are. I mean... God, Sam! She was young and *gorgeous.* They looked beautiful together... like they're on an episode of *The Bachelor* or some shit," I sighed irritably.

"Would you have felt better if she looked more like you?" Sam asked.

"Of course not!" I cried, then laughed out loud imagining someone like me opening the door. *How would I have felt?* "It was just the dose of reality that I needed before I said something that I couldn't take back," I added.

"Like that you love him and only want to be with him?" Sam laughed.

"Exactly!" I agreed loudly.

"Get your ass back there and tell him how you feel," she groaned.

"No way," I laughed like a loon. "He even called her 'love', Sam."

"I thought you said that's just a term of endearment," she sighed.

I groaned loudly. "Being away this week might help put things into perspective for me. Montana will be the perfect distraction. Plus, with Sam Walker coming up later this spring… I just need to stick to my original plan and not think about Erik for a while."

"So, you need a distraction from your distraction?" Sam sighed audibly.

"Exactly! We'll call it a diversion. Montana here I come…"

To be continued...

*** Keep turning for a sneak peek of Book Two in the
No Regrets series... *Diversion* ***

Elyse Rundell

acknowledgements

I've had stories rattling around in my head since I was a kid. Thank you to my husband who supported me and my wild decision to put them on paper. You are always my favorite distraction.

Thank you to my daughters, who are some of the greatest people that walk this planet. Y'all are my greatest accomplishment.

Thank you to my friends, some are even family, for laughing at my jokes and listening to my crazy stories. Y'all are my inspiration.

Thank you to my readers for joining me on this fun, limitless journey. It's just the beginning… so hold on to your boots!

Elyse Rundell

Sneak Peek

Will Kelly find a distraction from her distraction in Montana? If so, will it change her feelings for Erik? Here's a sneak peek of Book Two in the *No Regrets* series...

Diversion

"Hello," the blonde, lanky cowboy said loudly as he stopped next to me, tipping his hat, "Can I help you, ma'am?" He was cute, but I wondered if he was old enough to legally drink.

"Hi, handsome. I actually need a ride back to the Lodge. Could you help me out?" I smiled sweetly, though inside I was still as angry as a hornet at the bastard who was probably his boss.

"I sure can," he smiled now sporting a pink tinge to his cheeks, "hop in." I blew out a sigh of relief and climbed into the passenger seat of his ATV.

"Thank you!" I gushed and patted his shoulder. "I'm Kelly, staying here for the week. What's your name?"

"I'm LJ. Nice to meet you, ma'am," he said politely, his blue eyes sparkling as he smiled. "You said you needed to go to the Lodge?" he asked as he started driving.

"Yes sir. Your *'foreman',*" I said the last word with air quotes, "left me at my cabin even though he was told to bring me back... *God,*" I groaned, thinking about that bastard's handsome, punchable face and looked over at my young driver. "How do you put up with that asshole?"

"You mean Linc?" he asked with a chuckle. "He's not so bad. Just always down to business."

"Well, he needs to lighten up," I bristled. "How do you keep from punching him in his stupid face?" I punched the air in front of me and imagined it was Linc's nose.

LJ laughed out loud, "You have *seen* him, right? That big, solid son of a gun would lay me out with one punch!" I laughed along with the smiling cowboy, knowing he was one hundred percent accurate in that statement. Linc's forearm was probably as big around as LJ's thigh.

"Then I'll punch him for *all* of us," I offered, still punching the air like I was Rocky Balboa.

"Oh, hell no," LJ chuckled, shaking his head, "don't loop me into your plan. I happen to like all my body parts attached."

"Chicken," I mumbled to myself.

"Damn straight!" LJ retorted, making us both laugh. "Look, Linc doesn't like surprises or anything that gets his routine out of whack. He's a good guy, I promise."

"I'll try and reserve judgment, but it may be too late," I smiled. "Besides, it may be more fun to take a whack at his routine instead of him," I added with a sly, side-eye grin, making LJ chuckle.

"You're on your own with that," he laughed, shaking his head. We pulled up to the front of the Lodge and LJ stopped the Mule by the front porch steps. "Here you go."

"Thank you. I guess I'll see you around," I sighed as I hopped out of the vehicle.

"You will. Looks like Linc is inside... just so you know," he snickered, giving a nod toward the end of the porch where the other ATV was parked. "That's his Ranger." LJ tipped his hat at me as he drove away. I took a deep breath and opened the large front door of the Lodge; my anger having dissipated between toking up at my cabin and chatting with LJ. Walking inside the open room, I saw Carol smiling at me from behind the front desk with Linc casually leaning against the log pillar.

Good-looking bastard.

Elyse Rundell

Printed in Great Britain
by Amazon